8

Glacier
National Park

Going to the Sun

Adventures with the Parkers

STORY BY
Mike Graf

ILLUSTRATED BY
Marjorie Leggitt

FULCRUM
GOLDEN, COLORADO

J

Text © 2010 Mike Graf
Illustrations © 2010 Marjorie Leggitt
Photographs © Mike Graf: 1 (top), 5, 14, 15, 23, 28, 29, 32–33, 34, 39, 49 (all), 50, 53
(bottom), 56 (all), 58 (top), 64, 65, 66, 69, 75
© Shutterstock: Cover (all), title page, 1 (bottom), 3, 4, 8, 17, 18–19, 20, 22, 24, 25, 26
(all), 36, 37, 41, 45, 52, 53 (top), 58 (bottom), 63, 77, 84, 90–91, 93, 94, inside back cover
© Greg Lipinski: 60, 61, 68
Map page 80 courtesy of the National Park Service

Library of Congress Cataloging-in-Publication Data

Graf, Mike.
  Going to the sun : Glacier National Park / by Mike Graf ; illustrations by Marjorie
Leggitt.
      p. cm. -- (Adventures with the Parkers)
   Summary: Twin brother and sister, James and Morgan, embark on another adventure
with their parents to explore the history, unusual geology, famous sites, plants, and animals
of the Glacier National Park, where they learn about the threat climate change poses to the
glaciers there. Sidebar notes contain additional facts about the area and describe the park's
regulations and tourist facilities.
   ISBN 978-1-55591-671-8 (pbk.)
  1. Glacier National Park (Mont.)--Juvenile fiction. [1. Glacier National Park (Mont.)--
Fiction. 2. National parks and reserves--Fiction. 3. Vacations--Fiction. 4. Hiking--Fiction.
5. Global warming--Fiction. 6. Brothers and sisters--Fiction. 7. Twins--Fiction. 8. Family
life--Fiction.] I. Leggitt, Marjorie C., ill. II. Title.
  PZ7.G751574Go 2010

  [Fic]--dc22

                                        2009036170
Printed on recycled paper in the United States by Malloy Inc.
0 9 8 7 6 5 4 3 2 1

Design: Ann W. Douden
Cover image: Marjorie Leggitt
Models for twins: Amanda and Ben Frazier

Fulcrum Publishing
4690 Table Mountain Drive, Suite 100
Golden, Colorado 80403
800-992-2908 • 303-277-1623
www.fulcrumbooks.com

A large brown animal dove underwater.

Two calves nearby watched their mother disappear. One of the calves chewed on some water lilies, then searched around for more.

The other young calf turned back just in time to see a surge of bubbles break the surface of the marsh. The mother reappeared with a clump of pondweed in her large mouth. She slurped in the nutritious food as excess water drained away.

The cow moose hopped out of the water with her twin calves right behind.

One of the newborns slipped on the wet bank. It kicked at the ground, trying to get up. The mother returned to the water and approached the calf from behind, pushing it gently with her long snout.

Off in the forest, a gray animal tilted his muzzle toward the air and picked up a faint scent. He perked up his ears and took several steps toward the distant smell. The robust wolf trotted along, letting his senses guide him. He paused momentarily to lift his leg and urinate against a tree. Now other wolves would know where he had been.

The mother moose nudged at the struggling calf. The newborn bleated loudly and frantically kicked its feet. Finally, with the cow's prodding, the young moose stood up and wobbled along.

The three moose walked into a brushy meadow. In the middle of the grass was a flattened area. The mother and her two young lay down there. One of the calves rested its nose on the cow's stomach.

The area was surrounded by large sculpted mountains. Several small snowfields clung to the high peaks far above the trees. A few waterfalls cascaded down into the valley where the three moose rested.

The adult moose pivoted her ears in both directions, listening to the sounds of the wilderness. Then she, too, rested her head.

Several minutes later, the mother moose stood up. She led her young through a gently rolling stream. The delicate turquoise waters gurgled along rhythmically.

The lone wolf ran to the edge of the forest. He stopped and peered ahead toward a series of meadows and small ponds. The wolf paced back and forth, his powerful sense of smell alerting him that prey was very close.

Morgan, James, Mom, and Dad were cleaning up after dinner. It was their first evening in Glacier National Park in northern Montana. They were camped at Fish Creek, on the west side of the park.

Ten-year-old twins James and Morgan hoisted the ice chest into the car. "Be careful of Dad's banner!" Morgan whispered.

A ranger holding an animal pelt walked up.

Morgan and James put the cooler down in the trunk. Mom and Dad heard the approaching footsteps and looked up.

"Good evening!" the ranger greeted the Parkers. "Welcome to Fish Creek." The ranger glanced at the campsite. "You have one of my favorite spots in the campground. Just down the hill is a little trail leading right to the lake."

"We sure like it," Morgan agreed.

James looked at what the ranger was carrying. "What's that?"

"A wolf pelt," the ranger replied. She held it out for Morgan and James to pet.

Morgan reached over and touched the pelt gently. "What happened to it?"

"Unfortunately, this wolf was hit by a car," the ranger replied. "I'm giving a campfire talk on wolves tonight at the amphitheater so you can learn more about one of Glacier's predators. There won't be a fire, though. There's a burn restriction throughout the park due to the extremely dry conditions."

"What time's the talk?" Dad asked.

"7:30."

Dad glanced at his watch. "Fifteen minutes to finish cleaning up, then."

The ranger trotted off to another campsite.

The wolf crept slowly out of the cover of the trees. He reached the pond and quickly splashed across. Then he came to a flattened area in the grass and sniffed around, picking up a fresh scent. The powerful predator surged through the grass and crossed a gurgling stream.

The wolf saw movement ahead. He crouched behind a tree, growled softly, and bared his teeth.

"So," the ranger continued at the amphitheater, "wolves typically live in packs of about four to seven, although they can also travel alone. It often depends on the availability of food.

"Here in the West, they live anywhere from Alaska to Montana and in parts of Idaho, Minnesota, and Wyoming. Wolves are five to six and a half feet long and weigh eighty to a hundred pounds. They can be white, gray, tan, black, or multicolored.

"Years after their disappearance from Glacier," the ranger concluded, "they returned on their own around 1980. Now there are several packs living in the park."

The ranger pressed a button on her remote, and several pictures of wolves came up on the screen. She pressed another button, and a chorus of recorded howls serenaded the audience.

The crowd listened to the cacophony of calls. Mom leaned toward her family. "An eerie but beautiful sound if I've ever heard one," she said.

The ranger turned on the lights. "Thank you for coming to the presentation. I'll be up front if any of you want to ask a few questions or hang around and chat."

After the talk, Morgan, James, Mom, and Dad returned to camp. Dad looked up at the evening sky, then through the trees at Lake McDonald. "Why don't we head down there?" he suggested.

The Parkers walked to the sandy beach. They sat and gazed out at the placid lake.

A family of ducks paddled by. One by one they dipped their beaks into the water and lifted them back up. For a brief moment all five birds dove under at once. They resurfaced together a few feet away.

"I wonder if they're trying to catch fish," Morgan said.

"It sure appears that way," Mom said.

James studied the massive sculpted mountains at the far end of the lake. A small plume of smoke drifted above one of the peaks.

Sunset in Montana.

Dad glanced at his watch. "Nine o'clock," he announced. "And it's still light out."

"Welcome to northern Montana," Mom responded. "The land of late summer sunsets."

"It's completely dark at this time where we live," Morgan said.

"Except it's only eight o'clock in California," James reminded his sister.

A drop of saliva trickled out of the side of the wolf's mouth.

Sensing danger, the moose family began trotting away.

The wolf sprang after them.

One of the calves stumbled. Its wobbly young legs struggled to clamber over the rooty, rocky path.

The wolf bolted ahead, fixating on the trailing calf.

The mother led both calves toward a rock-and-boulder-strewn slope at the edge of a mountain. She turned and stood, shielding her young while nudging them higher onto the rocks.

The lone gray wolf closed to within fifty feet of the three moose. He dashed ahead while the calves scampered farther uphill, stopping where the mountain became steep.

The wolf ran right up to the moose family.

The cow turned her hind end toward the carnivore, hoisted her back legs off the ground, and kicked the wolf.

The blow slammed into the wolf's leg, sending him somersaulting onto the forest floor. He yelped, then stopped rolling. The wolf lay still, stunned by the kick. After a moment, he slowly stood. The wolf gingerly half-extended his paw and held it above the ground. A trickle of blood oozed down his leg. He licked the wound while keeping his eyes fixed on the three moose.

A moment later, he turned and hobbled into the forest.

The three moose watched the wolf limp away. Then the cow hopped up and nudged each of her calves down the slope. One calf stumbled and fell, knocking several rocks loose. More rocks gave way, creating a flurry of small boulders crashing down the mountain.

The mother instinctively bolted away from the building avalanche, her upright calf instantly following her. But the rockfall smacked into the sprawled calf. Debris quickly began burying her. Soon the young moose was out of sight. The cascade of rocks slowed to a trickle before finally stopping.

The cow moose bleated in distress. She climbed up the precarious field of loose rocks and pried and pawed at the rocks but couldn't get the large ones to budge. As darkness began to fall, the mother moose found shelter nearby with her remaining calf.

The Parkers rose from the sand and walked to a nearby footpath. They took the trail toward Rocky Point, a small, rocky peninsula of land jutting out into the lake.

After a few minutes, the family reached their destination. They circled the point, gazing at the shoreline and the views.

James heard something move in the forest. "What's that?"

They all peered into the trees, trying to decipher what it was.

"I don't see anything," Mom said.

Morgan heard the noise again. "There it is!"

The Parkers watched a ground squirrel dash across the forest floor and hop onto a tree trunk. The squirrel quickly scampered up the tree.

Dad gazed at the path toward camp. "You know, all that talk on our drive here has given us bearitis. Come on, let's head back." he said. "It's getting dark."

The next day, the Parkers packed up and drove north on a remote highway. The alternating paved and dirt road led them to the hamlet of Polebridge, just outside the northwest entrance to Glacier. Mom pulled the car up to a general store.

Dad got out and looked at the unusual little village. "I feel like we're in an outpost in Alaska somewhere," he said.

"Shall we check out the store?" Mom asked.

The family walked inside. The small store had groceries, souvenirs, and camping supplies. Morgan and James immediately noticed all the baked goods. They glanced at their parents, asking without saying a word.

"Don't worry," Dad mentioned. "I got hungry the moment I saw all those too."

The Parkers picked out some muffins and scones and sat down at a table.

After a night spent nearby the scene of the avalanche, the mother moose returned to her buried calf. She managed to flip a few additional rocks over. A partially mangled leg stuck up. The mother tried to dig some more while her other calf watched from a short distance away. The cow let out a final call of distress before climbing down to her remaining offspring. The two moose walked together toward the marshy pond that was their home.

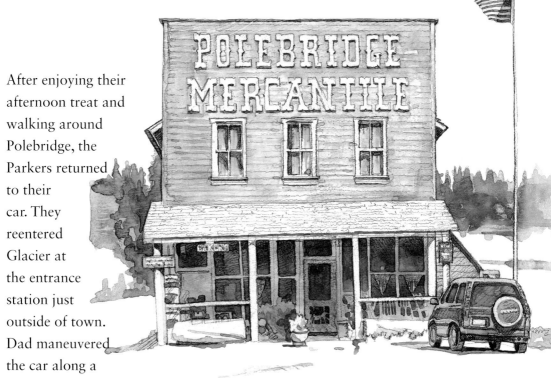

After enjoying their afternoon treat and walking around Polebridge, the Parkers returned to their car. They reentered Glacier at the entrance station just outside of town. Dad maneuvered the car along a rough gravel road. "It's definitely not a freeway out here," he commented. "I bet very few people come to this part of the park."

"But I'm glad we did!" Morgan exclaimed. "It's neat going to seldom-seen places."

Finally they reached the end of the road at Bowman Lake. Dad circled the small campground until the family found a spot they liked.

The Parkers paid for the site and set up their tent. Mom and Dad unhitched the kayak from the roof of the car. They hauled the boat toward the water's edge and plopped the craft down on the beach.

The family gazed at a long lake framed by deep forests and pinnacled mountains. "Wow," Dad exclaimed. "Now this is wilderness!"

The wolf stood up, stretched out, and licked his wound again. Then he gingerly hopped around in a small circle, carefully testing his weight on the injured leg. He immediately yelped and whined and lifted it again. Eventually the wolf limped back over to his makeshift den. He lay down and continued to clean the wound before resting his head on his paws.

Morgan and Dad took the kayak out first. They paddled away from the shore. Morgan noticed how long the lake was. "It goes on forever," she said to her father.

"It's like a fjord," Dad said.

"What's that?" Morgan asked.

"Fjords are long, fingerlike bodies of water carved by glaciers," Dad explained. "Only they're connected to oceans. These lakes in Glacier were also carved by rivers of ice, but freshwater filled them."

Morgan gazed at the high mountains. "Where are the glaciers now?"

"The big ones from the ice age 10,000 years ago are gone," Dad replied. "But the park does still have some small glaciers." Dad studied the mountains. "I imagine they're on the north- and east-facing slopes. Those areas get less direct sunlight, so the ice doesn't melt as fast."

Morgan and Dad paddled toward the forested shoreline.

"Look!" Morgan pointed.

Dad and Morgan watched a couple of people walking along the lake. Morgan gazed ahead to see where the trail led. She noticed something else moving. "There's an animal ahead of them!"

Morgan and Dad paddled closer. They approached the shoreline and surveyed the forest, then looked back to see where the hikers were. "At least if it's a bear," Morgan mentioned, "we're safe out here."

"Oh, I'm sure bears can swim if they want to," Dad replied. "But it's not a bear—look."

The animal lifted its head and chewed on some leaves. It walked into an opening in the trees before bending down and nibbling again.

"It's a deer!" Morgan exclaimed.

The moose and her remaining calf walked around the lake eating moss and grass.

Meanwhile, the odor of carrion filled the air.

High above the forest, a grizzly bear flipped over a large rock with her powerful front paw. She thrust her nose into the depression where the rock had been. The grizzly gulped down cutworm moths, then stood back up.

The bear detected the distinct smell of a fresh carcass. She scampered down from the boulder field and lumbered through the forest, turning over small rocks and digging up roots along the way. The strengthening scent of a dead animal directed her path.

Morgan and Dad watched the hikers pass by the deer. Then they paddled back to the beach. As they approached, Mom and James waded out into the turquoise waters.

James grabbed one end of the kayak and smiled. "This is what you get for being gone for so long," he said playfully. James and Mom started splashing Morgan and Dad, who used their paddles to splash back.

All four of the Parkers got soaked. After the water fight, they waded out of the lake, laughing, and returned their boat to camp.

Later that day, they decided to take a walk along the same trail the hikers had followed earlier. The path skirted the shoreline of the lake, moving through thick, dense forest along they way. The Parkers strolled along until they reached the Numa Ridge Trail junction.

Mom looked at her family. "Let's go a little farther," she suggested.

The Parkers continued hiking. The trail stayed in the shade of the trees, making it seem later than it was. Dad suddenly stopped and held out his arms. "Hang on a second," he announced. "Look at this."

Two large pieces of hair-filled scat were lying on the trail.

"That looks like dog poop," James said.

"Exactly," Mom responded. "Except dogs aren't allowed on park trails."

"Well, we know what does live in Glacier that is doglike," Dad said.

"Wolves!" Morgan remembered. She took a picture of the scat. "I'm going to check this picture with an animal identification book later."

The Parkers peered into the dark forest and back toward the lake. Mom glanced at her watch. "I can't believe it's 7 PM," she announced. "These Montana summer evenings really throw me for a loop."

Dad's stomach started gurgling. "Here I go," he commented. "One mention of supper time and I'm immediately hungry."

Eventually the grizzly found the boulder field with the buried calf. She homed in on the carcass and flipped away rocks and small boulders in her immediate vicinity. The large bear quickly unearthed the dead animal.

The grizzly stuck her muzzle into the moose and ripped into the flesh. The powerful bear stood up with fresh meat dangling from her mouth.

Meanwhile, the wolf tilted his head up. A whiff of meat aroused his senses. The wolf's stomach growled and hunger overcame pain. He stood up and hobbled around. Then the wolf set out, limping toward the scent.

As the Parkers approached the campground, they could hear people. "It's kind of comforting to have other campers nearby," Mom admitted.

They stopped at the beach where they had launched their kayak earlier. Dad walked toward the shoreline. "I want to take in the view once more," he explained.

Bowman Lake at twilight was ethereal and mysterious. In the distance, layers of spired peaks were silhouetted against the hazy skies. Dense forests hugged the shoreline. Morgan snapped several photos.

"It's quite a place," Mom commented.

"But you can tell there's a forest fire burning," Dad added. "The visibility just isn't what I'd expect."

Then hunger got the best of the family, and they trudged back to camp.

The wolf came to the edge of the forest. He peered out and saw a grizzly bear pawing away at a dead animal. The wolf bared his fangs and quietly snarled. He took a few cautious steps toward the bear.

The grizzly stopped eating. She sniffed the air, then stood on her hind legs while bobbing her head back and forth.

The wolf crouched down and stared at the upright bear, and at the carcass next to her. After a moment, the wolf turned and trotted away.

The next day the Parkers broke camp at Bowman Lake.

They drove back down the gravel road, through Polebridge, and eventually returned to the south end of the park.

At Apgar, Mom turned the car northeast. The family drove past the long and densely forested shoreline of Lake McDonald, heading toward the park's high peaks. Eventually Mom pulled the car into Avalanche Creek Campground.

The Parkers drove around and chose an open, flat spot surrounded by tall trees. They set up, then packed for a hike up to Avalanche Lake.

The first part of the trail was on a wooden walkway through a dense cedar and hemlock forest. The Parkers strolled along, admiring the large trees and reading signs about the old-growth forest and how Native Americans used the trees to make boats and other supplies.

At the end of the boardwalk, the family approached a railing overlooking a narrow gorge cut by a rushing stream. They stopped there and peered into Avalanche Gorge.

"That's a beautiful little mini-canyon," Mom said. "And look at the ferns growing right out of the rock walls where it stays cool and moist all the time."

The Parkers admired the gorge for a few minutes before continuing on.

After two miles of trekking through the forest, the family made it to Avalanche Lake. They stepped off the trail and onto the lake's pebbly

shoreline. Morgan, James, Mom, and Dad gazed at the aqua waters surrounded by cliffs and high mountains. At the far end of the lake, several waterfalls cascaded from above.

Mom pulled out the binoculars and looked all around. She noticed people at the lake's opposite end. "Let's head over there," she suggested, "and have a little picnic."

After eating again, the grizzly used her paw to shove dirt over the carcass. Then she walked up to an open, grassy slope.

The bear stepped into the meadow, glanced back at her cache, looked all around, then sat down.

Meanwhile, the smell of carrion continued to waft into the air. The wolf, unable to resist, again trotted toward the scent, saliva dripping from his teeth.

When the wolf reached the clearing, he spotted the partially buried carcass in the distance, but the grizzly appeared to be gone. He limped cautiously toward the food, unburied the stash, and quickly ripped off a small piece of flesh.

The grizzly, sensing an intruder in the vicinity, lifted her head. The large bear sniffed the air and recognized the scent of another predator. She plowed through the brush, heading back to the carcass.

The wolf heard the bear first, then saw it crash through the bushes.

As the bear ran up, the wolf backpedaled, then circled around and dashed at the bear's rear end, nipping at the grizzly's hindquarters and pulling out a tuft of fur. The bear turned and charged the wolf, but the intruder hopped backward and managed to keep his distance.

The wolf closed in again, biting away another chunk of fur from the back end of the bear. The bear whirled and chased the wolf several yards away toward some trees.

Then the grizzly returned to her food. The wolf cautiously followed, again trying to nip the bear's behind.

This time the bear whipped around and swiped her paw at the wolf, catching the intruder and giving him a glancing blow across his side with her sharp, powerful claws.

The wolf yelped and stumbled several feet, then jumped away and hobbled into the forest, leaving the bear and carcass behind.

Later, with several miles between him and the bear, the wolf stopped next to the roots of a large tree. He licked the gashes on his side, lay down, then tended to his new injuries some more.

Eventually, the large grizzly flipped the calf's jumbled bones. She looked them over before walking away. The bear then began a long trek toward Glacier's high country and the east side of the park, where the sweet taste of berries awaited.

Back at camp, the Parkers munched on cookies while darkness engulfed the dense forest. "It sure is quiet around here," Mom said.

Dad glanced up from his book. "I do miss having a fire."

"Me too," Morgan added. "It makes hanging out at camp feel safer."

The wolf tilted his head up and howled. After a few more calls, the injured canine whimpered, then lay down for the evening.

The next day the Parkers got off to an early start.

The road east of Avalanche followed McDonald Creek. Far above, a solitary peak spiked high into the air. Its snowfields glistened in the morning sun.

James stared at the picturesque mountain, then checked his map. "It's Heavens Peak, I think."

"How high is it?" Morgan asked.

"8,987 feet."

Mom suddenly slowed down the car. "Well, if we have a little bit of heaven up there, look at what we have down here."

Right in the middle of the road was a large, fresh-looking pile of bear scat.

"Hmm," Dad pondered as he gazed into the forest. "I wonder how far away the culprit is."

A large bird with a white head circled far above the marsh. It spiraled upward on the morning's rising warm-air currents, gliding along until it spotted something below.

The eagle slowly drifted down.

Suddenly, it tucked its wings and quickly descended, landing on the limb of a tree.

The bald eagle gazed at a jumbled mass of bones.

The bird hopped from its perch and found a piece of stringy leftover tissue and tugged at it with its beak. The elastic tendon stretched out, causing the eagle to hop back. Finally, the meat ripped off the bone and the raptor devoured it.

A raven landed a few yards away. It tilted its head sideways and eyed the carcass. The black bird hopped a few feet closer.

The eagle squawked and spread its wings, then stared at the intruder.

The raven hopped closer to the hoof of the calf, at the opposite end of the carcass. The smaller bird began pecking away at this part of the dead animal.

Soon, another raven joined the feast.

Mom slowed the car again. Two bicyclists were stopped ahead. They straddled their bikes as they peered forward.

Morgan saw why the cyclists were stopped. "Look, a bear!"

The black bear sat in the middle of the highway, far ahead of the riders. It stared at the two people, and they stared back.

Mom pulled up right behind the cyclists while Dad leaned out the window. "How long has it been there?"

One of the riders turned his head halfway. "We've been here about ten minutes, and it hasn't budged."

A car approached from the opposite direction. The black bear turned around and rambled into the forest.

The cyclists looked at each other. "I guess we should go now," one said.

"But what if it's right behind those trees?" the other replied.

Mom heard the conversation. "We'll escort you," she called out.

Mom drove slowly past the cyclists so they could follow. As the group crept by the place where the bear had disappeared, everyone peered into the woods, looking for the large animal.

After a few minutes, one of the cyclists gave Mom a thumbs-up sign. She waved to them and sped up, leaving the bikers behind.

The Parkers continued on, reaching a large bend in the road called The Loop. The road climbed steadily, Heavens Peak looming in the west.

James leaned forward from the backseat. "You can see the road up there."

"All the way until the gap near the top," Dad added. "Just like the road is heading toward the sun."

CLIMBING TO THE SUN

Going-to-the-Sun Road is the main highway in the middle of Glacier National Park. It takes visitors up over Logan Pass and through some of the most spectacular scenery in the park. The road is named after nearby Going-to-the-Sun Mountain.

Up to eighty feet of snow can accumulate on Logan Pass, forming what's called the Big Drift. Because of deep, late snows and poor visibility, the road takes about twelve weeks to plow in the spring. Logan Pass is usually open from mid-June to mid-October.

Before the road was finished in 1933, it took visitors three to four days to get across the park.

The road climbed on, hugging a cliff on the right. A small stone wall protected drivers from a long tumble should they accidentally veer off course.

Mom maneuvered carefully around a bend. "This is quite a road!" she exclaimed.

The family passed a long, continuous shower of water cascading onto the highway. "The Weeping Wall," Mom announced, reading the sign.

Across the way, a plume of water fell below several peaks and snowfields. The Parkers passed a sign pointing it out as Bird Woman Falls.

Morgan leaned forward. "Is that snow above the falls a glacier?"

"It's hard to tell from here," Dad replied. "Can you see what the map says, James?"

But James was staring at something far above. He studied the two distant objects until he saw one of them move. "There are two animals up there!"

Morgan tried to look out James's window. "I want to see too."

Mom took a quick peek then said, "I really need to keep an eye on the road." She noticed a turnout ahead. Mom pulled over and the Parkers scrambled out of the car.

James pointed up the mountain. "There they are!"

The two animals were perched on a rock, gazing down on the road.

"What are they?" Morgan wondered aloud. "They're light brown like some grizzlies, but much smaller."

"Are they cubs?" James asked.

Dad grabbed the binoculars and focused on the animals. "I see," he announced. "They're not bears at all."

Dad passed the binoculars to Mom. Mom took a look. "Marmots!" she exclaimed.

The Parkers gazed at the perched rodents. Just then, the two cyclists slowly huffed by. Dad noticed sweat dripping down their faces. "How's it going?" he asked with concern.

"It's quite a climb," one of the riders replied between breaths.

"And we have to be at the summit before 11 AM!" the other added.

"Do you need anything?" Dad asked.

"Thank you, we're okay," the first cyclist responded.

Dad got into the car and looked at his watch. "It's 10:30," he said. "I hope they make it."

"Why do they have to be at the top by then?" James asked.

"The park wants all cyclists off the winding west side of the road by eleven because the traffic gets too heavy after that."

The family piled back into the car, and Mom continued driving toward the summit. As she approached the cyclists chugging along, a car passed going the opposite direction. Mom slowed down, staying behind the riders. "There just isn't any extra room on this road!" she exclaimed.

After the car passed, Mom inched by.

Morgan leaned forward and spoke to Dad. "Are you sure you want to ride this road?"

"I'm sure I want to try," Dad replied. "But I'm thinking of going east to west. There's less traffic on that side of the park."

The Parkers drove the last stretch before the pass. They passed a small parking area and a cascading waterfall. At the summit, several cyclists were dismounting their bikes. They leaned them up against a sign that said Logan Pass 6,646 feet elevation. One of the bikers took a picture of their whole group.

Mom pulled the car into a crowded, busy parking lot, and the Parkers climbed out. James noticed the hazy, smoke-filled skies to the east. "It must be a huge fire," he said.

The wolf lay among a series of tree roots deep in the forest. He licked his injuries again, but didn't try to stand.

Two squirrels scampered about in the forest nearby. A high-pitched call signaled some intended meaning from one to the other.

One of the squirrels frantically dashed down the trunk of a tree. It scurried across the forest floor with the other running after it. The lead squirrel jumped onto the base of another tall pine. The two squirrels chased each other in circles, spiraling up the trunk until they reached the upper branches of the tree. One began nibbling a cone, dropping the shavings onto the forest floor. Soon the other was chasing after it again, both scampering down the tree and onto the ground.

The scrawny, famished wolf kept still while staring at the unsuspecting squirrels as they ran right toward the carnivore. He tensed and waited, then pounced, landing with his paw on a squirrel's back. The wolf pinned the squirrel down and bit off its back end, swallowing the whole chunk. The other squirrel dashed away, wailing, into the trees.

The wolf chomped further into what was left of the squirrel. A few quick bites, and the whole animal was gone.

The grizzly crossed an alpine region of grasses and tiny flowers along the Continental Divide. The bear rambled across a small, melting glacier.

Eventually she meandered down from the alpine zone. Far below, a deep, cobalt blue lake glistened in the sun. The lake was dotted with small floating chunks of ice.

The grizzly noticed people sitting on rocks near the lake. She gazed at them, watching for movement, then continued downward until she entered a forest filled with thick shrubs.

A clump of red berries caught the bear's attention. She wandered closer and lifted a paw to bend the shrub toward her. The grizzly opened her mouth and swallowed a cluster of tiny, sweet fruits. Then she stood up and searched around for more.

The grizzly rambled from one buffalo berry patch to another, devouring as many of the delicacies as she could find. Then she paused from her feast and sniffed the air.

Far below her were a sow and two cubs. The large bear watched them for several minutes as they, too, fed among clumps of bushes, then she dropped down and foraged for more berries.

The Parkers joined a small group of people behind the Logan Pass Visitor Center. A ranger was standing on a rock, giving a talk. "Thousands of years ago, immense rivers of ice carved both sides of the park," he said, then pointed east. "We know that because of the massive U-shaped valleys.

"And because of the glaciers' impact," the ranger continued, "the park was named after them. In the 1800s, there were at least 150 glaciers here. Now, due to climate change, only about twenty-five are left."

The ranger turned and looked at the mountain behind him. "Clements Mountain used to have one of those glaciers. But it expired around 1938. The current projection is that all of the park's glaciers will be completely gone by 2020. They are rushing to oblivion.

"But global warming affects more than glaciers. It can change meadows, raise tree line, and alter food sources for animals. And although it may be too late to save the glaciers here, we can all consider changing our habits to reduce pollution, which is heating up our atmosphere."

The ranger ended his talk, then stayed around to answer some questions.

The Parkers began their journey toward Hidden Lake.

"So," James said, "whatever glaciers we see on this trip, we may never see again."

"Unless we come back real soon," Morgan replied.

"I want to see as many as possible, then," James announced.

"Me too," said Dad.

The Parkers trekked up a series of wooden steps. Soon they approached a large mound of rocks near the foot of Clements Mountain.

"There's the old moraine from the glacier," Dad realized. "It's where the ice pushed the rocks before the glacier receded."

The Parkers gazed at the alpine scenery. Wildflowers filled the meadows off the boardwalk. "Look at all the bear grass stalks," Mom said. The tall white flower was splashed throughout the meadow.

"Are they named that because bears eat them?" James asked.

"More because they grow in typical bear habitat," Mom replied.

The family looked around. A cascading stream tumbled down from the moraine. Nearby, a small patch of snow still clung to the ground. But there were no bears.

On the way to Hidden Lake.

Soon the family left the boardwalk and began hiking on a dirt path. Morgan noticed a group of people peering toward some stunted trees. Several of the hikers had their cameras out.

A large white animal emerged from the shrubs. "A mountain goat!" Morgan exclaimed.

The large goat, whose fur was matted, walked slowly along. A smaller goat followed it. The adult turned and charged the smaller one, running right across the trail.

"Whoa!" Mom exclaimed as the wild animals brushed by.

The two goats slowed down by a clump of trees.

"Hey! Over there!" James exclaimed.

The other mountain goats were farther up. One was walking right on the trail. Dad watched it. "Those things have some seriously strong leg muscles," he commented.

"I guess they need them to climb these mountains," James said.

BORN TO CLIMB

Adult mountain goats are three to four feet tall and weigh between 150 and 300 pounds. They eat alpine grasses, flowers, hemlock trees, and shrubs. Mountain goats are well adapted to living on rocky cliffs. Their hooves have special pads that give the animals traction and prevent them from skidding. The pads act like suction cups on the rocks. A mountain goat's hooves have hard, sharp edges surrounding a soft inner area. The two halves of a mountain goat's hoof can move separately from one another. This helps the goat get a better grip while climbing.

Once the animals moved farther away, the family scurried by and came to a wooden platform overlooking Hidden Lake.

The Parkers gazed at the deep blue lake and the mountains all around it. Across the way was pyramid-shaped Reynolds Mountain. In the opposite direction, James noticed a slab of ice atop a peak in the distance. "I think that might be part of Sperry Glacier!" he exclaimed.

"Our first glacier sighting," Morgan announced. "Although we can't see much of it from here."

They eventually made it down to a sandy area along the lakeshore. Mom and Dad passed around snacks. Morgan remembered her journal. She took it out and wrote:

Dear Diary:

I'm writing from Hidden Lake. We've seen a bunch of mountain goats along the trail, and a few minutes ago a mountain goat and its kid walked right up to the lake, about ten feet away from us! We watched them as they lapped up some water.

They were so close we felt bad. I know we aren't supposed to be near the park's wildlife. But it's almost like they are tame. And they're everywhere around here. I can even see tufts of their fur caught on some branches nearby.

I LOVE Glacier! I can't wait to see some of the park's glaciers up close.

Hopefully some of the smoke from the fires will be gone soon too, then we'll get the deep blue skies we're expecting.

Sincerely,

Morgan

Morgan and James rolled up their pant legs and took off their shoes. They waded into the shallow water of Hidden Lake. "You guys should come in," James said to his parents.

Mom dipped her toes into the water. "You know," she concluded, "I think it's at kids' temperature, not adults'!"

We found Hidden Lake!

The family spent the night camped at Rising Sun.

They got up the next day under hazy skies. After eating breakfast, the Parkers packed up for a long hike.

They walked to the shuttle bus stop next to the campground. "It's nice to leave the car behind," Dad said as he sat down on one of the shuttle seats and stretched out.

"And it reduces pollution," Morgan added, since these buses run on biodiesel.

The Parkers got off at Siyeh Bend and began their ten-mile hike. They climbed steadily into a region filled with small trees and wild-flowers. Soon they crossed a footbridge over a cascading stream.

A man with a day pack approached the family on his way down. "How's it going?" he greeted them.

"Great!" Dad responded. "And you?"

"Well, Siyeh Pass is one of my favorite trails. You're in for a real treat."

James looked at the man questioningly. "Have you seen any bears?"

"Not today. But I did see *that*!" He pointed to the west. High up on a mountain was a large, lone slab of ice that glistened in the sun.

"Is that a glacier?" James asked.

"I believe so!" the man replied and took off down the trail.

Mom unpacked the binoculars and focused in on the snowfield. "It looks like a glacier," she reported. "There are cracks in the ice. And it's in a perfect spot, high up on an east-facing slope."

"Our first full look at a glacier in the park," James announced with satisfaction. He pulled out his map. "It must be Piegan Glacier."

The Parkers gazed at it for a while, then hiked on, moving into an alpine zone of meadows and stunted trees.

Morgan turned around to look at the small glacier once more. "The views just keep getting better and better!" she exclaimed.

Soon the trail changed from dirt lined with small alpine plants to loose rocks skirting the side of a mountain. Dad paused at a small patch of snow blocking the path. He stepped onto the ice where others had walked previously and guided his family carefully across.

"We should be close to the summit now," he reported.

Fierce, gusty winds whipped about. Finally, the trail turned a bend and leveled out. The Parkers stopped and leaned against the rocks for a moment.

"We're on top of the world!" Mom exclaimed while peering down.

"Siyeh Pass!" Dad announced as the winds buffeted his jacket. "8,150 feet, and the highest-elevation trail in the park."

They walked a few steps down from the pass and stopped at a circular pile of stones. Morgan directed her family to stand near the summit marker. Then she looked for a place to set her camera.

A high-pitched squeak came out of nowhere.

James hurriedly looked around. "What was that?"

A tiny furry animal stood nearby on a small rock, a clump of grass in its mouth. The animal stared at the Parkers, its whiskers quivering.

The little creature whistled again, then dashed into a hole.

"It's a pika," Mom said. "It's part of the rabbit family. They only live in high alpine regions."

The Parkers heard another squeak just as a shadow fell on them from above. Mom glanced upward. "Aha!" she exclaimed. "Now I know why they are warning each other."

Morgan, James, Mom, and Dad watched the drifting bird.

"I think it's a bald eagle. See its white head?" Dad said.

The large bird dipped toward a giant slab of ice below the mountaintop.

"Hey!" James exclaimed. "There's another glacier!"

Morgan hurriedly got her family in place to take the picture. Then James pulled out his map and unfolded it. "That one's Sexton Glacier," he announced.

"Look at the chunks of ice and their cracks," Dad exclaimed.

"And that waterfall below it," Morgan added.

"Well," Mom concluded, "this trail sure is full of wonderful surprises."

The Parkers began a long trek down a series of switchbacks. Sexton Glacier, with its distinct chunks of ice, stayed in view.

Soon the family was back among a few tiny trees. A short spur trail led toward the glacier. The Parkers took it, stopping to sit on some rocks with a view of the whole slab of ice in front of them.

After eating lunch, the family returned to the main trail and continued to hike down. "I'm sure glad we're not going up this!" Morgan mentioned.

Finally, the Parkers worked their way back into the forest.

The trail approached a red rock gorge containing several small waterfalls. Mom gazed at the cascading stream. "This place is amazing," she said. "Every section of trail is so spectacular and full of surprises."

Eventually the sound of cars replaced the rushing stream. "We're almost back to the road," Dad said.

Just before the highway was an overlook at Sunrift Gorge. Morgan, James, Mom, and Dad stared into the straight-walled canyon with a stream running through it. A few minutes later, pleasantly tired from their hike, they walked down and caught the next bus to their campground.

Later that evening, the family drove a few miles east. Dad pulled the car into a small parking area called Two Dog Flats. The family piled out and stared up at a sloping grassland. Beyond the grass, the area turned to forest. On the other side of the road, St. Mary Lake stretched over several miles. Haze and smoke filled the air.

Morgan scanned Two Dog Flats. "Nothing's out there now," she reported.

The Parkers continued watching patiently. Mom started walking onto the grass with James, Morgan, and Dad following her.

In his peripheral vision, James suddenly noticed a small, gray animal up the hill. "There's something out there," he called out softly.

The doglike animal limped downhill from the flats toward the road. The Parkers stood still and breathlessly watched as he approached.

Mom leaned toward her family and whispered, "I think it's a wolf. It's gray and larger than a coyote."

Morgan studied the animal with the binoculars. "It's hurt!" she realized.

The wolf hopped across the road right in front of the Parkers. Morgan tried to quickly snap a few photos. Once the carnivore crossed, he stopped and licked his injured paw, then carefully loped toward some trees.

"Welcome aboard, everyone!" a ranger called from the deck of the boat. "We're now crossing Lake Josephine. Do you notice how the water here is a little turquoise?"

A crew member quickly walked up to the ranger. He whispered something to him and pointed to the forest next to the water. The ranger glanced in that direction, then looked again. He turned toward the passengers and announced, "Folks, we're going to take a little detour and warn some hikers along the trail."

Morgan looked at James. "I wonder what's going on."

The boat turned toward the shore. A crew member handed the ranger a microphone.

Morgan, James, Mom, and Dad watched through the boat's windows. Several bushes moved near the trail. James spotted the bulging back of a large brown animal. "It's a bear!" he realized.

Suddenly Morgan noticed that a group of people were hiking toward it. A shiver went up her spine.

The ranger put the microphone to his mouth and waited until the boat got a little closer. "There's a bear ahead of you!" he announced into the PA system. The ranger called out again. "There's a bear up ahead! It's below the trail, near the lake."

The hikers stopped and turned toward the boat. One person cupped his hands and called back. "What kind?"

"A grizzly!"

The hikers looked at each other and began talking. The people on the boat watched, wondering what they were going to do.

Several more hikers caught up to the first group. Slowly, the large gathering of people proceeded. A person in the front yelled out, "Hey, bear!"

At the top of a small hill, the group stopped. The bear was down below, a short distance off the trail. A distinct hump on its back curved up between its shoulders.

The bear heard human voices. It glanced toward the boat and at the group of people on the trail, then returned to foraging for food, seemingly unaffected by their presence.

The hikers quickly scooted past the grizzly.

The ranger watched until the group appeared to have safely gone by. He stepped back inside. "That was a close call. But the hikers did the right thing. They stayed together and made sure the bear knew they were there."

The boat crossed the rest of Lake Josephine, docking to let the passengers on the Grinnell Glacier guided hike disembark. They walked across the dock and gathered together on the shore.

"Good morning, bears!" The ranger called out into the forest loudly, startling some in the group. Then he turned to everyone. "I'm ranger Rick," he introduced himself. "By the way, does anyone know how to tell the difference between black bear scat and a grizzly's?"

No one answered.

The ranger smiled. "Grizzly scat has bear bells in it!"

Everyone laughed nervously.

Rick explained. "There's no better way of alerting bears than our voice. Bells could make a bear curious. They might sound like a pika or marmot—bear food. We certainly wouldn't want that!"

One person with a walking stick removed the bells from his pole.

"I'll tell you about a bear encounter I dealt with along this trail in a little while. But first, I want to mention that there's safety in numbers, and we're a large group. Though we need to be careful, keep in mind that you're going on one of the prettiest hikes in the park, and to a very interesting place too."

Rick started walking down a path. He cupped his hands and announced in a deep voice, "Yo, bears. We're here!" Then he turned to the group. "Come on! We've got a lot of trail ahead of us."

Farther along, Rick waited for the forty or so people to gather.

"Okay. Let me point out a few things. The large mountain in back there is Mt. Gould. In front of it is Angels Wing. What's left of Grinnell Glacier is between those two peaks. And down below is one of the real jewels of this park, Grinnell Lake. We'll continue to see it and its great display of turquoisity along the way."

A little while later Rick stopped the group near a series of red rocks. He removed his cap and wiped some sweat off his face. "It's an awfully warm day," he said. "But that's been the trend these last few summers. Years ago it hardly ever got this way so high up in Glacier. And the winters have warmed up significantly too."

He turned around and pointed. "Even Gem Glacier, near the top of the mountain, has bare ice on it now. This has only happened in the last couple of years. Usually the ice is covered from last winter's snows."

Rick looked straight down at Grinnell Lake. "One day that jewel of water will lose its turquoise color. And unfortunately, that day isn't too far off But I'm getting ahead of myself. Now I want to tell you my bear story.

"A few years ago, on this very trail, a woman and her father took off to Grinnell Glacier early in the morning. They were the first ones on the path that day. Just ahead of this spot they climbed around a bend and a grizzly and cub were right on the trail.

"One of the most dangerous things you can do is to surprise a sow and her cub. The grizzly charged and attacked. Both the daughter and father tumbled off a cliff. This seriously injured them, in addition to their wounds from the attack, but it also might have saved them."

Rick paused to catch his breath. "I was the ranger on duty that day. And let me tell you, it was one long day. A hiker came running down to tell me what happened. Well…I've never hiked up this trail so quickly. I got to the two people and radioed for help. We had to fly them both out in a helicopter, but they survived. In fact, the father came back a year later to hike this very same trail!

"One thing we should all consider when hiking in bear country is to go in large groups, like we are today. But enough of this scary bear stuff," Rick said, turning back toward the glacier. "You can only see the top of Grinnell Glacier now, so let's hike the rest of the way and look at all of it. And by the way, George Bird Grinnell discovered Grinnell Glacier back in 1887. It's been extensively viewed and studied ever since."

Morgan and James noticed the bear spray clipped to Rick's belt.

Mom saw where James looked. "We're going to have to get some bear spray for ourselves," she mentioned, keeping her family close behind the ranger.

The group passed a waterfall splashing vigorously onto the trail. The Parkers, like the other hikers, dashed by, hoping not to get soaked. Eventually, everyone reached the last group of trees before the final steep climb.

Someone noticed an animal nearby. "Look. A bighorn!"

The large, noble-looking sheep was standing on a mound of rock, its thick horns curling over its head.

"There's another one," Morgan called out.

"They're guarding the valley," Rick announced with a smile.

The group proceeded up the trail. As they passed the bighorns, Morgan and James counted. "I've seen twelve so far," James reported.

The path began to level off. One last large sheep was perched on a huge boulder, staring down at the hikers.

"He's right above us," Dad whispered nervously as the family dashed by.

Finally the group reached the top. Straight ahead was a remnant arctic scene. Grinnell Glacier was full of cracks and large chunks of ice. Some icebergs were floating in a small turquoise lake. A waterfall splashed down from Salamander Glacier above it.

Suddenly a booming, cracking sound rumbled up from the ice field. It echoed throughout the mountain bowl like thunder. The Parkers and the whole group froze and looked all around.

A cascade of small boulders and rocks showered

onto the glacier from the cliffs above. Then a large chunk of ice broke away and tumbled into the lake.

The newly formed iceberg dipped below the water and bobbed and weaved its way to the surface. A series of rippling waves followed, flowing toward the shore.

Slowly, the free-floating chunk of ice steadied. Rick turned toward the group, grinning. "Well, you don't get to see that every day!"

Once everything appeared stable, Rick presented more information. "We used to lead our hikes onto the glacier itself. Obviously that can't be done anymore because of the lake. Come here, everyone, I want to show you some pictures."

The group gathered around while Rick held up a poster. "This is the park's Boulder Glacier in the 1930s." Rick's picture showed the tongue of the glacier with a large ice cave in it.

"And here it is now." The next photo showed the same area, completely barren of ice and snow.

Rick held up another picture. "Here's Grinnell Glacier years ago. Notice how it was attached all the way up to Salamander Glacier."

"Wow," a person in the group exclaimed. "It really has lost a lot of snow."

Someone in the group raised her hand. "What makes it a glacier and not a snowfield?"

"Excellent question," Rick replied. "A snowfield is formed by more snow accumulating than melting. If the snowfield continues to grow each year, it eventually gets large enough to move. That's when we call it a glacier. Usually they have to be 90 to 100 feet thick to start moving. When glaciers lose ice mass and stop moving, they are no longer glaciers.

"I'd like to have a couple of young, strong volunteers for a demonstration," Rick said next.

The group looked at Morgan and James, the only children on the walk. "Perfect!" Rick said, following the group's eyes. "Would you two mind helping me out?"

Grinnell Glacier

1930s

Today

Morgan and James stepped up. Rick handed each of them two small stones. He kept a pair for himself. "What I'd like you to do," Rick explained, "is take the sharp edge of one rock and scratch it as hard as you can against the other. Do this over and over until you form a powder."

Morgan and James each put their flat rock on the ground. They held it steady with one hand and rubbed the sharp rock back and forth on it. Meanwhile, Rick also rubbed his two rocks together.

After a minute, Rick stopped and caught his breath. He looked at Morgan and James, still working away. "Okay. That looks good." The twins carefully picked up their rocks and stood.

Rick turned to the group. "What we've just done on a very small scale is what glaciers do." Rick glanced at Morgan and James. "Rub your hand over the scratched area on the rock."

All three of them did this. "Now, let's hold up our hands."

Morgan, James, and Rick showed their palms. A fine powder covered their skin.

"One cubic foot of glacial ice weighs nine times more than the same size block of regular ice or snow because the glacial ice is compressed. And when glaciers move, they grind the rock underneath them into a rock flour like we just made. That rock dust is so light, it floats in water. When sunlight shines through it, it causes glacial lakes and streams to have a turquoise color—just like this lake and the larger Grinnell Lake below."

"Hey, we saw a little bit of that at Avalanche Lake," Morgan whispered to James.

"How about a hand for our glacier simulators here!" Rick called out, and everyone clapped as Morgan and James walked back to their parents.

Rick wrapped up his talk: "This awesome glaciated place won't have these glaciers much longer. Global warming is changing all that. But we'll still call it Glacier because of the scenery the glaciers created. Thank you for joining me on the hike. If you go back on your own, just remember to warn the bears along the way."

Dad looked at his family. "Let's hike down with the group," he said, giving the kids a wink.

The grizzly huffed along, climbing far above the trail. A large pile of sand and pebbles piqued her curiosity. The bear lumbered over and noticed tiny black insects scampering out of a hole on top of the mound.

The bear stuck her nose into the hole and licked up a bunch of ants. Then she furiously pawed at the top of the massive colony. A flurry of ants rushed out of their disturbed home. The grizzly lapped up as many as she could. Some of the ants managed to find their way onto the bear's face and fur. A few trickled into her nose.

The grizzly hopped back and shook her head vigorously. She swatted at her nose several times, then sneezed and huffed while backing farther away from the mound. She shook her head and rubbed her nose on the ground. Finally, the bear rolled her face and body onto a nearby pile of dirt.

Somewhat relieved, the grizzly stood up and shook her whole body. She glanced at the ravished ant mound and lumbered away.

The Parkers chatted with Rick on the way down. When they reached the junction to Grinnell Lake, Morgan, James, Mom, and Dad said good-bye.

Soon they had left everyone behind and the Parkers were alone, hiking in a dense forest. Dad led the way. "Hey, bear!" he called out while trying to imitate Rick's deep voice.

They saw people ahead of them, and the Parkers purposely caught up. Now nine people snaked their way through the forest toward Grinnell Lake.

Someone in the front stopped. "Look out up here," she warned. The woman stepped cautiously over a large pile of fresh scat and shouted, "Bears! We're coming through!"

Morgan glanced at the scat as she walked by. She noticed tiny pieces of red berry scattered throughout it.

They reached a footbridge hanging low over a stream. One by one they crossed the swaying bridge and gathered again on the other side.

Finally a clearing appeared between the trees. Morgan, James, Mom, and Dad walked onto a sandy shoreline. Straight ahead of them was jewel-like Grinnell Lake.

The Parkers sat down next to the water. James quickly pulled out his journal.

This is James Parker reporting.

I'm sitting here at Grinnell Lake in Glacier National Park. This lake and the one above are different from others. They're turquoise because of Grinnell Glacier.

But it's not just the water color that makes this lake fantastic. There's a huge waterfall across the way that comes from the glacier. And there are incredible mountains all around us. Rick said Native Americans called Glacier's mountains "the backbone of the world." Now I can see why.

What's really sad, though, is that the color of this lake will change back to normal in about ten years. That's when Grinnell and all of the park's other glaciers are expected to have melted away due to global warming.

But it's still exciting seeing glaciers, and we've gotten a good look at five so far: Piegan, Sexton, Gem, Salamander, and Grinnell.

Speaking of exciting, we have Dad's little surprise coming up soon. I don't think he has any idea it's coming!

Reporting from Glacier,

James Parker

After a few more minutes at the lake, the Parkers packed up. They returned to Lake Josephine and stopped at the junction.

Mom turned toward her family. "Do you want to hike back the rest of the way or take the boat?" she asked.

The family thought about the bear they saw earlier in the day and the scat on the trail.

"Let's take the boat," James blurted out.

"Definitely," Morgan added.

Later that evening, after cooking dinner at their site at the Many Glacier Campground, the family walked over to the nearby Swiftcurrent Motor Inn store. A large group of people were gathered in the parking lot with binoculars and telescopes.

Rick was among them. He saw the Parkers. "Hey, it's my buddies from Grinnell Lake! How was the rest of the hike?"

"Fine," Morgan replied.

"No bears?"

"Only scat."

Rick pulled a pair of binoculars off his neck. "Do you want to see a grizzly now?"

"Yes!" Morgan exclaimed. She took the binoculars first. "Look at that grassy slope halfway up the mountain," Rick directed. "To the right of a tree is a small brown dot. But it's moving."

Morgan scanned the area where Rick pointed. "There it is!" she called out.

"There's also a cub nearby," Rick mentioned.

Morgan passed the binoculars to James. James focused in. "The cub is just below the mom," he reported.

After Mom and Dad took a turn, they handed the binoculars back to Rick. "Now that's the way to see a grizzly," Dad said, "from a nice, safe distance."

The Parkers said good-bye to Rick and then strolled over to the store for some ice cream.

Mom and Dad clipped the bear spray canisters

they had purchased the night before to their belts. The family gathered their lunch and water and walked to the nearby parking lot. At the end of the lot was the Iceberg Lake Trail.

The Parkers began their early morning hike on a worn pathway.

As the family walked along, they heard dogs barking.

Dad stopped and looked around. "That's weird," he said. "Dogs are usually not allowed on national park trails."

Farther up the trail was a ranger with a large group of people. They were all gazing into the brush. Suddenly the group gathered close together. A moment later they began coming down the trail toward the Parkers.

The family watched the line of people hastily descend. The ranger spoke into a handheld radio as he walked.

The first person in the line of hikers approached the Parkers. "They're closing the trail," he reported.

"How come?" Mom asked.

"We just got bluff-charged by a grizzly. Apparently there's also a mother and her cubs farther up the trail."

Morgan, James, Mom, and Dad filed into line with the others. They hiked out with the large group, eventually spilling into the parking lot. Three people with dogs on leashes were at the trailhead.

"I guess there *are* dogs out here," Morgan said.

The Parkers stopped and waited for the ranger, to ask him what was going on. Finally he approached from the back of the line. Morgan was the first to realize it was Rick.

"Hi!" she greeted him.

Rick waved, then stopped to put down his pack. He took out a sign and posted it at the trailhead.

Danger: The area beyond this sign is closed due to bear danger.

Mom stared at the ominous message. "I'm glad we got the warning!"

"We've been monitoring this trail all summer," Rick explained. "It's prime grizzly habitat, and the buffalo berries are ripe. We've had to close it before, and I'm sure we'll have to again."

"How long until it's open again?" Dad asked.

"That I'm not sure about. We'll need at least three days of grizzly-free trail first."

Rick looked at the people with the dogs. "I'm glad you and your canine friends were still around," he said to them. "Are you ready for some bear conditioning on the Iceberg Lake Trail?"

A woman in front nodded. Rick, the dogs, and their guides hiked up the closed trail.

The Parkers walked over to the bench in front of Swiftcurrent Motor Inn. They sat down and looked out at the parking lot. "I wonder what they're going to do with those dogs?" Dad pondered.

After a few minutes, James looked at his family. "Well, since we can't hike here, what do you want to do?"

Mom pulled out a park newspaper and sifted through it. "Hmm. This could be interesting." Mom explained her idea.

"That does sound like fun," Morgan, James, and Dad agreed.

The Parkers walked over to their campsite. They put the bear spray in the bear locker and drove out of the park. At the junction, Dad turned north and they were on their way to Canada.

The highway paralleled the park. Soon, a solitary, square-sided mountain dominated the view. "That's quite a peak," Dad commented.

James searched for the mountain on his map. "It must be Chief Mountain," he reported.

● ● ●

The dogs sniffed around a large paw print in a muddy section of trail. They picked up a scent and started following it.

Soon, the dogs and their trainers came upon a large, solitary grizzly foraging nearby. The dogs barked furiously and tried to rush at the bear. The guides held the dogs in place and watched.

The grizzly heard the commotion and looked up.

One of the guides called out brazenly to the grizzly: "Hey, bear. Go on, bear. Get out of here."

The bear stared at the group. Then it continued searching for food.

One guide led the group a few steps closer. She commanded, "Bear, you get out of here now."

Still the bear was slow to move. The woman turned toward Rick. "It might have gotten human food somewhere around here in the past. It's harder to work with food-conditioned bears."

Rick looked concerned. "That's unfortunate."

While the dogs barked incessantly and kept their leashes taut, the guide called out again, but the bear stayed in the vicinity.

"Well, here's our next step," one guide said. She pulled out a special rifle and checked to see that it was loaded. Then she aimed the weapon at the ground below the bear. "Okay, here goes." The guide shot several rubber bullets near the bear.

The bear took off and rambled into the bushes until it was out of sight.

"Good bear!" the guide called out. She immediately turned to the dogs. "Okay, quiet now," she commanded, and the dogs became silent.

Rick turned to the group. "What next?"

"We keep on conditioning the bear until it no longer needs dogs or rubber bullets to avoid humans," the guide explained. "Their reward is to get away from the chaos we bring them. I'm confident this training will work."

The group watched the spot where the bear disappeared. "Let's check again later," a guide said, and they trotted down the path, looking for other bears in the area.

BEAR SHEPHERDING

The Wind River Bear Institute in Montana trains and works with Karelian bear dogs to help teach bears in Glacier and other areas to avoid humans. They call this bear shepherding. The purpose is to make wilderness areas where people and bears cross paths safe for humans. In the long term, this is also best for the bears. By using dogs, voice commands, and at times rubber bullets or firecrackers, institute members teach the bears that humans are a nuisance and should be avoided. The bears are taught to leave an area only when humans are around; they can return to feed later. Karelian bear dogs have been used since 1996 in wilderness areas in hundreds of situations. No dogs, humans, or bears have been hurt in the process.

Eventually the Parkers went through customs and entered Canada. They wound their way into Waterton Lakes National Park, Glacier's twin park in Canada.

Dad drove into town and found the marina. He parked the car, and the family climbed out. They got tickets and found their seats just as the ferry left the dock.

After a while, a person spoke into the sound system. "Welcome to Waterton Lake," the guide announced. "We're on the largest of Waterton's three main lakes and the deepest lake in the Canadian Rockies. Waterton Lake is 487 feet deep.

"Waterton-Glacier is the world's first International Peace Park. The two parks joined to become a peace park in 1932."

The boat slowed to a stop right in the middle of the water.

"Look at the mountains on each side of the lake," the guide directed. "See anything unusual?"

James noticed a strip cut out of the forest. *What happened to the trees?* he wondered.

"Welcome to the 49th parallel," the guide said. "And back to the United States. The trees are cut along the border every fifteen years, all the way to the ocean."

"So we're back in Glacier now," Morgan realized.

The boat sped up and continued cruising. A short time later it slowed down again as it approached Goat Haunt, then docked. The Parkers got off the boat with the rest of the visitors. They all proceeded down an asphalt trail toward a ranger station. A US park ranger met everyone there, checked IDs, and asked some questions before letting them back on US soil.

US–Canada border.

The Parkers waited by a sign with a small group of others. "I like this guided walk thing," Mom said. "We learn about the park, and we don't have to fend for ourselves in bear country."

Ranger Lynn Dixon trotted up and introduced herself. A moment later the small group was hiking toward Kootenai Lake.

Lynn set a brisk pace on the mostly flat trail. A short time in she stopped and let everyone gather around. "Notice this pile of pulpy, dry nuggets. Does anyone know what animal did this?"

"Elk?" James wondered.

"Deer?" Morgan asked.

"Moose," Lynn answered. "We're on the trail of the moose. You'll see why soon.

"This scat is from last winter. The moose eat almost all wood then, because sticks and bark are about all they can find above the snow."

A few minutes later Lynn stopped again. "Moose," she informed the group, "actually crossed over the Bering Strait from Asia about 150,000 years ago. They settled in Alaska, Canada, and Maine—all areas above the 50th parallel. We're at the 49th here. They began to inhabit this area 150 years ago. Does anyone know why?"

Nobody had an answer.

"They came on their own," Lynn answered. "They moved into these 'spruce-moose' forests, or so we call them, where forested areas

Kootenai Lake.

had been cleared by logging and beavers had built dams. The dams made marshes and lakes that moose love."

The group hiked farther down the trail. At one point, Lynn turned and said, "Male moose can have antlers up to six and a half feet wide. Those antlers are the fastest-growing bone in the world, growing up to a half inch a day! Moose can also weigh up to 1,200 pounds. They have powerful legs that move straight up and down when they run. That might make them have an awkward gait, but it also helps them pull up out of the snow. And there's plenty of that around here in the winter. Moose can also withstand temperatures down to –48 degrees! The hollow hairs that make up their shaggy fur keep them warm.

"In summer, when grass and leaves are abundant, they can eat up to fifty pounds of food a day. They'll sometimes dive underwater to get food. And they love to swim. We've even seen them paddling across Waterton Lake!"

Lynn started walking briskly forward. "Kootenai Lake is just around the corner."

Soon the forest gave way to a body of water with marshy grass surrounding it. The group stepped out of the trees and started scanning the area. James noticed a large animal wading in the distance. "A moose!" he pointed.

"And there's her baby," Morgan added.

The mother moose dipped her head into the marsh and came up with a mouthful of soggy grass.

Lynn whispered, "I've seen moose every time I've been to Kootenai Lake this summer. This mother had two calves until recently. We don't know what happened to the other one. It's common for their young not to make it through their first year. They're a favorite food of grizzlies.

"Moose calves grow extremely fast. They're about 22 pounds at birth in the spring and 220 pounds by the end of summer. They stay with Mom all winter, and after a year, she'll try to kick them out, just like human parents do with their grown kids." Lynn laughed. "Some refuse to leave, though.

"Go ahead and wander along the shore," Lynn said. "Just stay far away from the moose. They're very unpredictable and are known to charge humans. And one more thought," Lynn added. "A Native American legend says that if you dream of moose, it means you'll live a long life. So tonight I hope everyone dreams of moose."

The Parkers watched the gangly ungulate and her calf in the picturesque surroundings.

A short time later, everyone regrouped and retraced their steps to Goat Haunt with Lynn.

As they returned to camp that evening, Dad turned the car into the Many Glacier Hotel parking lot. The family got out and gazed in awe at pinnacled peaks and pyramid-shaped mountains silhouetted against the horizon. Dad let out a sigh, "What an amazing place."

The family wandered into the hotel and out the back door onto the deck. They spent a few more minutes there, watching the slow sunset and the onset of twilight from the hotel's deck. Many other visitors were doing the same thing while also taking pictures.

Then the Parkers walked downstairs and joined an evening program.

The lone wolf tilted his head up and let out a series of howls. He then perked up his ears and listened for a reply from within the darkening forest.

Another wolf, somewhere, answered his call. The injured wolf howled again and slowly trotted forward before suddenly coming to a halt.

Across the way, two glowing eyes stared into his. The two wolves gazed at each other from a distance, their tails upright and fur rising.

The wolves walked cautiously forward until they were close enough to touch. They began circling and smelling each other. Their tails remained standing, but the fur on their backs settled down.

After a few minutes, the wolves walked off together, one limping, toward the forest.

Morgan, James, Mom, and Dad tore down camp

early the next morning. They left the Many Glacier area and headed south. At St. Mary, Dad turned the car back into the park and drove west on Going-to-the-Sun Road.

Eventually the Parkers pulled into the Lake McDonald Lodge parking lot. They packed snacks, extra clothes, flashlights, bear spray, and water. A shuttle bus took them back to Logan Pass. Then another brought the family down to the Gunsight Pass trailhead.

The Parker family stepped off the bus along with a couple of other hikers, hoisted on their day packs, and Dad announced, "Here we go, the grand finale of our trip!"

James looked at Dad. "And we don't have to carry all our camping gear."

"The chalet's going to be a real treat," Mom said.

"And our car will be waiting for us at the end," Morgan added.

The Parkers began their journey by traversing a gentle, forested slope. Soon they came to a junction. A sign leading to a backcountry campsite said:

Danger: The area beyond the sign is closed due to bear activity.

The Parkers read the warning just as a couple caught up to them.

"Hmm," Dad murmured, his hands automatically reaching for his bear spray canister. "Let's not hang out here, okay?"

They hastily hiked on. The couple stayed close behind. "Mind if we tag along?" one of them asked.

"Of course not," Mom replied. "We did the same thing the other day at Grinnell Lake. We're much safer in numbers here in bear country."

Morgan noticed that the man and woman were only carrying day packs. "Are you staying at the chalet too?" she asked.

"We are," the man replied. "By the way, I'm Greg, and this is my wife, Corinne."

"I'm Morgan, and this is my twin brother, James. My mom and dad are Kristen and Robert."

A marshy stream meandered along on the east side of the path. James noticed its turquoise-colored water. "There's a glacier somewhere up there!" he announced with enthusiasm.

Dad caught a glimpse of a bush shaking up ahead. He paused and held out his arms until everyone stopped. "Hey, bear!" Dad shouted.

"What did you see?" Mom asked nervously.

"I'm not sure yet."

Dad inched forward.

A squirrel jumped off the bush and scampered across the forest floor. It leaped onto a tree and hurriedly climbed it. From a high branch, it looked down on the intruders, twitched its tail, and blared a shrill-pitched call.

"I guess we disturbed it," Corinne concluded, chuckling at their nerves.

Soon the group came to another junction.

They all sat down and ate snacks. Morgan had Corinne take a picture of the whole family on the wooden footbridge.

After a few minutes, Mom stood up. "We should move along. There's still lots of hiking ahead today."

"We're going to take this short side trail to Florence Falls," Greg said. "Thanks for letting us hang with you."

"No problem," Dad replied. "Maybe you'll catch us on the way up. If not, we'll see you at the chalet."

The Parkers trekked on, climbing a ridgeline with views of ice-laden peaks in the distance.

The wolf's new companion trotted up with a dead animal in her mouth. She dropped the squirrel right in front of the injured wolf.

The carnivore stood up and put his foot down on the rodent. He quickly tore into it with his sharp teeth, pulling away a section of meat.

Mom pulled out the binoculars. The family took turns inspecting the chunks of glacial ice on the mountains ahead.

James took a quick peek at his map. "I think those are the Jackson and Blackfoot glaciers," he said.

The family heard footsteps approaching from above. They looked up and saw a solitary ranger striding down the path.

"Beautiful trail," Mom said to the ranger.

"I know. I love it!" the ranger agreed. "Is everything okay?"

"We're fine," Mom responded.

The ranger trekked on, her equipment rattling as she walked.

The Parkers soon reached the top of the ridge. They continued on through a wildflower-filled meadow with clumps of trees scattered here and there. The family soon approached the Gunsight Lake backcountry campsite and stopped at the cooking area to snack and use the privy. Morgan noticed a group of packs dangling from bear poles nearby. "Look," she pointed.

Just below Gunsight Pass.

Dad looked at the surroundings. "It must be great to camp out here!"

"As long as you're careful with your food," Mom replied, smiling.

Their path took them to the lake. At a small footbridge they gazed at the scenery spread out before them. Gunsight Lake sat in a deep mountain bowl framed by high peaks, snowfields, and cascading waterfalls. Dad picked out a faint line indicating the trail toward Gunsight Pass. "Major climb ahead!" he announced.

James examined the snowfields clinging to the high peaks. A few of them had noticeable cracks in them. He checked the map. "I wonder why those aren't glaciers."

Dad thought for a moment. "It might be they're not big enough. Remember, they need to be about 100 feet deep to move."

"And twenty-five acres wide," Mom added, recalling something else Rick had mentioned.

Mom noticed dark clouds building up. "We better keep moving," she prompted. The Parkers began the long climb as a light mist started sprinkling down. They trekked on, alternating between warm and sweaty because of the climb and cold from the light rain and dropping temperature.

The trail switchbacked steadily until it was high above Gunsight Lake. Soon the family was looking down at the deep, U-shaped valley that held the large body of water. "Boy," Dad said in awe, "the ice age glaciers around here must have been huge."

The narrow trail hugged a cliff, with steep drop-offs plunging all the way to the lake. Across the way a melting ice field's plume of water plunged out of its base, zigzagging down a rocky ridge.

The Parkers kept climbing. A tongue of ice appeared far above on their left. Large chunks of blue ice hung precipitously down from it. "Glaciers or not, there's a lot of ice around here," Dad said.

Morgan took several pictures of the hanging ice field to their left and Gunsight Lake far below. Then she gazed down at the path they had climbed and saw two people. "Greg and Corinne are coming!" she exclaimed. Morgan waved to them. They saw her and waved back.

James counted all the streams of water plunging down from the snowfields. "There are at least eight waterfalls around here," he announced.

Soon the trail leveled off. The family splashed through pools of water and a waterfall that soaked the trail. They tramped over a remnant patch of snow and past displays of delicate alpine wildflowers.

Morgan noticed a structure ahead. "There's a building!"

Morgan, James, Mom, and Dad surged on. Finally they made it to Gunsight Pass.

Mom noticed that James was shivering. "Let's get inside and try to warm up," she said with concern in her voice.

The Parkers walked into the small stone storm shelter and Dad pulled the door closed. The family sat down, put on more clothes, and pulled out some snacks.

After a few minutes, James glanced out the window. The clouds hung low over the mountains as a light rain drifted down. "It's really getting wet out there," James announced.

The wooden door to the shelter slowly creaked open, then stopped. Morgan, James, Mom, and Dad turned to look. The door opened a few more inches. The Parkers traded nervous glances.

A small animal walked inside. It looked at the family and twitched its nose.

Dad scolded the marmot. "Go on. Get out. There's no food for you here."

The marmot stayed put.

Dad stomped his foot, then took a few steps toward the alpine creature.

The marmot turned and scampered out.

This time, Dad latched the door. "That ought to keep our animal friends out."

The Parkers huddled close, still trying to warm themselves.

A moment later the latch to the door popped up and the door started to creak open again.

The family stared at the door, bewildered, wondering what animal had the dexterity to enter.

Greg and Corinne stepped in and saw the Parkers. "Hello, old friends!" Greg called out.

"We thought you were another marmot," James replied. Then he explained what had happened a few minutes earlier.

Soon the rain abated and the sun began to peek through the clouds. All six hikers stepped outside. They worked their way down a series of steep switchbacks and past a gushing waterfall on the other side of the pass.

The trail now paralleled Lake Ellen Wilson. It started climbing again. The weary but content hikers trekked on.

Finally, after another long climb, the trail topped out at Lincoln Pass. The group gathered there and gazed at large Lake McDonald in the hazy distance. Morgan scanned the area directly below. "There's the chalet!" she exclaimed.

"Boy, that's a sight for sore eyes," Corinne added.

Everyone clambered down and reached their hotel in the wilderness a short time later. The Parkers quickly checked in.

Morgan opened the door to their room and peered inside. She turned to her family. "There's no place like home!"

The Parkers had three beds in their rustic quarters. Morgan, James, Mom, and Dad quickly pulled off their shoes and wet clothes, hopped into their beds, and got under the covers. "I'm exhausted," Mom exclaimed.

"And cold," James added through chattering teeth.

The dinner bell rang an hour later. Dad quickly sat up. "I'm suddenly hungry," he announced.

Mom laughed. "That's no surprise."

The family walked toward the dining hall and found their assigned table. Greg and Corinne were already there.

The staff from the chalet stood in front of the
dining hall. They introduced themselves and gave guests tips for their visit.

The kitchen manager spoke last. "This is my fifth summer here
at the chalet. I came years ago as a guest, like you, and decided this is
where I wanted to spend my summers. One thing I've learned is not to
leave any wet clothes hanging outside. The mountain goats may end up
eating them."

I'M GOING TO SWITZERLAND!

When Glacier was first encountered by European explorers, they called it the Swiss
Alps of America. Sperry Chalet and its nine sister chalets were built starting in 1911.
The chalets were modeled after Swiss architecture, and an Italian stonemason
used local rocks to construct the stonework. Sperry Chalet opened as a hotel in
1914. In their prime, these chalets often hosted more than 100 people a night. All
the chalets closed during World War II. They were run by the railroads, which at that
time diverted their resources to the war rather than tourism. Most of the chalets
were eventually torn down. Only Sperry and Granite chalets are still in operation
today, and one other in the Two Medicine area has been converted into a store.

"Before we eat, let's go around and have a person from your party
introduce your group," said the manager.

People from each table stood up, told where they were from, and
shared some thoughts about Glacier National Park. Guests came from

Minnesota, Texas, Spain, Washington, Montana, and Florida, among other places.

Finally, everyone turned to the Parkers' table and Greg stood. "My name is Greg and this is my wife, Corinne. I'm an airline pilot, so we get to travel often. We're from Chicago, but we used to live in Montana. It's no exaggeration to say that Glacier is our favorite place on the planet."

Greg sat down and looked at the Parkers. Morgan got up and introduced her family, then continued. "We hiked over Gunsight Pass today. My parents said it's one of the best hikes they've ever done. James and I agree. But we might all change our minds tomorrow when we hike to the glacier!"

The manager smiled at the guests. "Our food is brought up regularly all summer by horse train, and we had a shipment delivered today. You must all be famished. Dinner is now served!"

After a meal of pasta, green beans, soup, and bread, Morgan, James, Mom, and Dad played cards with Greg and Corinne. Eventually they wandered outside to the deck to enjoy the sunset under now-clear skies. Far below, Lake McDonald glistened in the sun.

"What time are you heading up to the glacier tomorrow?" Corinne asked the Parkers.

"Right after an early breakfast," Mom answered, "so we can take our time on the long trek down to our car."

"We'll see you somewhere on the trail, then," Greg replied. "We're going to sleep in and start later. We're staying two nights here at the chalet."

The late Montana sunset lit up the sky as the evening began to chill. Morgan and James zipped up their jackets just as the sun finally dipped below the mountains.

The wolf pair trotted out to Two Dog Flats. They scanned the open plain and spotted a herd of elk.

The wolves casually trotted toward the herd. The gray wolf still limped, but he managed to keep up with his new companion.

The predators crept closer and studied the elk. They noticed a small calf on the fringe of the group.

The wolves charged straight at the calf.

The elk perked their ears up and saw the rapidly approaching predators. They immediately dashed away, disappearing into the nearby trees.

The two wolves ran in and out of the forest, searching for the elk. They found them all bunched together with the calves in the middle of the pack. Eventually the wolves regrouped, worked their way down the slope, and crossed the road. Finally the pair left the Two Dog Flats area and St. Mary Lake altogether, heading toward the southern part of the park.

The chalet visitors headed inside. The wooden guest quarters were cool and dark. Morgan, James, Mom, and Dad each turned on a flashlight, changed into pajamas, and climbed into their beds.

Mom pulled the blankets up and held them snug against her chin. "It's certainly cozy in here!" she said.

"Good-night, everyone," Morgan called out from her bed.

"Good-night!" James chimed back.

In the morning after breakfast, the Parkers began their hike toward Sperry Glacier. The trail immediately steepened, and as they trudged up it, James paused to see how far they'd come. "It seems like we're hiking toward the sky," he said with delight.

Morgan heard a pika whistle. She briefly saw the tiny animal dash away from the trail. "It does look like a little rabbit!" she called out to her mom.

James pointed to a cliff above them. "There's a bigger animal up there!"

A mountain goat was perched on a rock.

It appeared to be watching the Parkers hike.

After a series of steep switchbacks, the pitch of the trail eased.

The family now passed several mossy, gardenlike areas with trickling waterfalls and small ponds. Finally they reached a larger lake with a snowfield sticking up out of it. Its blue ice shone through the water at the lake's edge.

Mom gazed at their surroundings. "And I thought yesterday's trail was magnificent. This is unreal!" she cried, awestruck.

The trail steepened again. It soon led directly into a narrow slot in the rock wall. Morgan, James, Mom, and Dad peered up into the opening at a series of cemented rock stairs. A cable was bolted into the stones for hikers to hold on to.

"The rock staircase," Dad recalled. "I remember reading about this."

One by one, the family hauled themselves up the stairs. They regrouped at the top, where it was breezy and noticeably cooler.

The Parkers gazed in wonder at the massive slabs of ice and chunks of glacier to their left and right. In the distance, the largest of the ice fields loomed. "Wow!" Dad gasped. "This is even better then I expected."

Morgan took several photos at Comeau Pass. The Parkers noticed small rock piles, or cairns, indicating the path to the main part of the glacier. Morgan, James, Mom, and Dad trekked on. They climbed a finger of rock, then dropped down to a tongue of ice, crossed it, and climbed again. At the top of each mound was another cairn with a post in it. The Parkers kept hiking.

Finally, Dad noticed a small weather station, its anemometer, for measuring wind speed, spinning in the breeze. From there, the Parkers stared at the largest remaining part of Sperry Glacier. The mass of ice dipped down from the mountain with a distinct set of cracks near the top.

James looked at his father. "Let's climb Mt. Everest next!" he said enthusiastically.

Dad put his arm around James. "It does seem like we're doing that type of an excursion, doesn't it?"

Mom took a deep breath. "It's hard to imagine this glacier being gone in ten or so years. It's still quite large."

The family found a place to sit down and study the scene. Below the glacier, a couple of turquoise ponds were filled with its meltwater.

James pulled out his map. "I think," he checked again, "that below those ponds is Avalanche Lake, where we were the other day."

"Doesn't that seem so long ago?" Mom mused.

A crackling, tumbling sound came from the ice. Across the way a few small rocks had broken off a cliff and rolled onto the glacier. The rocks soon stopped and settled on the bare ice. Then all became quiet again.

Morgan fished through her day pack and pulled out her journal.

Dear Diary:

Here I am at one of the largest remaining glaciers in the park, Sperry Glacier. To me the area seems like a construction zone. There are piles of rock and ice all over. And it's quite a sight to see. I wish we could have been here when all these separate pieces of the glacier were still together. The glacier would have been huge then!

I would also like to see some of the other glaciers in the park before it's too late. Speaking of coming back, that's what a lot of people at the chalet have done. I guess Glacier really draws people. Maybe I'll work at one of the park's chalets in the summer when I get older.

Anyway, we have to go back down the trail—all the way to Lake McDonald. It's going to be a _long_ downhill journey, so we have to get going soon.

Sincerely yours from Sperry Glacier,

Morgan

The Parkers looked over Sperry Glacier once more.

Mom glanced at her family. "I guess we better skedaddle."

They began their trek back.

Along the way, James kept sniffing. Morgan looked at her brother. "Are you crying?"

"No, cold," James answered. "But I have to admit, I am sad. I wish I could see this glacier every day."

As they started to climb down the rock stairs, Greg and Corinne were heading up. The Parkers stopped and waited for them at the top.

"Welcome to the rooftop of the world," Mom announced.

James pointed ahead. "Wait till you get up there."

"We're on our way!" Corinne said.

Morgan, James, Mom, and Dad continued down. Eventually they returned to the junction near the chalet. The Parkers hiked on, heading toward Lake McDonald, far below.

They reached their car in the late afternoon.

After checking in to the lodge at Lake McDonald, they showered, ate dinner, and went to bed early. It had been a long day.

The next morning, James opened his eyes and checked to see if anyone else was awake. His dad's snoring assured James they were going to hang around in their room at least a little while longer.

After a few minutes, James quietly pulled out his journal. He tiptoed outside, sat down in a chair on the porch, and wrote:

> This is James Parker reporting.
>
> My family and I are basking in the safety and comfort of a cabin at Lake McDonald. My mom says we deserve this after the hike we were on.
>
> But what a hike it was! We saw glaciers, waterfalls, and high mountain lakes, all surrounded by sculpted glaciated peaks. Dad says it was like walking in a postcard. I know I'll never forget it.
>
> So here we are with a few more days left in the park, but I'm not sure what we'll do. We found out yesterday that the fires are spreading. It's kind of weird, because this park is known for glaciers and ice.
>
> Anyway, I better go see if anyone's rustling out of bed.
>
> Reporting from Glacier,
>
> James Parker

The grizzly lumbered along, finding stray ripe berries here and there. Many branches had been stripped during the feeding frenzy of the last few days.

The bear heard human voices far below.

The grizzly found a rock and stood with her front legs propped on it to look. She saw a large group of people snaking up a path. The grizzly rambled up the mountain, getting far away from the voices.

At the northern end of the park, a few leaves blew on top of the half-buried moose calf's bones. Flies buzzed around and landed on rotten pieces of flesh. Beetles and maggots crawled on the carcass, eating the remains.

Eventually Morgan, Mom, and Dad all managed to get up. They moved slowly while packing. Dad lifted a duffel bag and arched his back. "Man, I'm sore," he said.

"You're getting older," Morgan replied with a mischievous smile.

After checking out, the family ate a hearty brunch of omelets, French toast, pancakes, and potatoes at a restaurant nearby. Then they crossed Going-to-the-Sun Road once more, seeing several mountain goats near the summit.

Mom pulled the car over at the St. Mary Falls trailhead. "Shall we give this a try?" she asked her family. Dad got out and stretched and yawned. "It's only a short trail," he reassured everyone.

The Parkers hiked slowly to the falls. Once there, they stood on a footbridge and admired the churning aqua water as it roared out of its gorge toward St. Mary Lake.

After a few minutes, the family tromped back, stopping at a sandy beach along the way.

Mom found a place to sit, and she spread out a large blanket. They spent the next couple of hours hanging out next to the lake. Morgan and James took an occasional dip in the water while their parents rested and read.

Fresh, dark smoke continued billowing up from just over the mountain. Soon the sky became even more obscured. "We should probably go," Mom announced, looking at the orange-ish haze across the horizon.

They returned to Rising Sun Campground and found an empty site. After setting up their tent, Mom and Dad made pasta for dinner.

Afterward, Dad studied the smoke-filled skies. "This is really sad, how bad the fires are. What the park needs is a good rain. And that doesn't appear to be in the forecast."

Later that evening, Dad pulled out his bike. Mom saw Dad tinkering with it and quickly stood up. "I'm going to get some supplies at the lodge store." She walked over to Dad and kissed his forehead. "I'll be back in a few minutes."

Dad put the wheels back on his bike and checked the derailleur and brakes. He oiled the chain while Morgan and James watched.

"Are you looking forward to the ride?" James asked.

"Absolutely. Going-to-the-Sun Road is supposed to be one of the best rides anywhere. That's why I brought the bike."

Morgan asked, "When are you leaving?"

"Right after sunrise. I want to beat the traffic."

Dad pumped up his tires, then locked the bike to the picnic table. Just then a ranger walked up. "How are you folks doing?"

"Great," James replied.

"What's up with the fires?" Dad asked.

"We're watching their progress and trying to control them. It's a daily battle we've been fighting for weeks now. There are multiple fires in and around the park to deal with." The ranger noticed Dad's bike. "I see you're getting ready for a ride."

"Yeah, up Going-to-the-Sun Road," Dad answered.

"Well, it's best to go early," the ranger suggested. "There are fewer cars and typically less smoke in the morning. But keep your eyes on the sky and know we will be too in case any emergencies come up. Hope you have a great ride!" The ranger trotted off to visit other campers.

A few minutes later, Mom returned and hastily put the groceries in the car. Eventually the Parkers piled into their tent.

• • •

At 6 AM Dad's cell phone alarm played an inspirational song. Dad squirmed out of his sleeping bag, grabbed the pile of clothes he had laid out the night before, and began crawling out of the tent.

Mom held up Dad's cell phone. "Are you going to take this?" she asked.

Dad turned and paused for a second, thinking. "No," he replied, "I haven't been getting good reception in the park."

After changing into his riding clothes in the car, Dad slipped on his biking shoes and unlocked the bike. Then something in his peripheral vision caused him to look up.

Morgan, James, and Mom were standing there, waiting to send him off.

Dad glanced at his watch. "I should be back in about three hours," he estimated. "Somewhere around nine."

"Be safe," Mom said. "Have fun!"

"Bye, Dad," Morgan and James added.

Dad hopped onto the saddle and began pedaling. He waved to his family before disappearing down the road.

As soon as Dad turned onto the highway, he began climbing.

As Dad pedaled along, St. Mary Lake glistened on his left and a dense forest hugged the road on his right.

"Hey, bear!" Dad shouted into the forest between breaths.

The morning sun was warm, and Dad was sweating. A plume of dark smoke billowed up from the mountains to the east of St. Mary Lake.

Dad pushed harder as the grade steepened. He felt as if he was moving in slow motion. Dad started to feel a tiny bump each time his back wheel made a complete circle. It got worse and worse. Finally, it increased to the point that he could no longer ignore it. He looked down. "Oh, no!" Dad mumbled to himself.

Dad pedaled on, trying to avoid the inevitable. He rounded a bend just as his back wheel started thumping loudly.

To his dismay, Dad saw a pile of fresh bear scat right in the middle of the road. As Dad rode slowly parallel to it, he could see pieces of undigested red berries sprinkled throughout the droppings. "Hey, bear!" Dad shouted with renewed anxiety.

Dad again glanced down at his back wheel. His tire was now completely flat. He had no choice but to stop.

He quickly pulled over right across from the scat. Dad gazed into the forest. "Hey, bear! Just fixing a flat. Don't mind me!"

Dad pulled the hand pump off the bike and attached it to the valve on the back tire. He pumped vigorously, then stopped. A distinct whistle of air escaped from the inner tube.

Dad pulled the pump off and felt the tire. It was flat again.

Working quickly, Dad pulled some small tools from the pouch beneath his seat. He took his back wheel off the bike, pried off the old tire, and yanked out the flat tube. Dad inspected the tire for thorns or glass but couldn't find anything. He grabbed a new tube from the pouch and pumped a tiny bit of air into it. Just as he fitted the tube into the tire, he heard a car approaching.

The car slowed down, and the driver rolled down the window. "Is everything okay?"

"Yes, I'm fine. I just got a flat."

"Well, you might not want to hear this, but we just saw a bear."

Dad stopped working and looked at the driver. "What kind?"

"A black bear."

Dad laughed. "I wonder if it's the same one that's been pooping on the highway."

The man glanced into his rearview mirror. He saw another car coming down the road. "I better get going," he said. "Are you sure you're okay?"

Dad nodded, and the man waved as he pulled away.

Dad hastily finished putting in his new tube. He fit the tire back on and quickly pumped it up. Dad put away his tools and glanced into the forest just off the road. "Hey, bear," he called again, "I have to go now!" He hurriedly got back on his bike and resumed his climb. "Boy, that's a relief," he said to himself.

The two wolves stood on top of a ridge. They gazed at tongues of red flames licking the sky above the forest.

An unusual whock, whock, whock *sound came from above. The wolves looked up and saw an object fly overhead toward the nearby inferno.*

The helicopter opened up from the bottom. Water poured out, just missing the two animals as they scampered away.

Dad pressed on, pedaling past landmarks he was now familiar with. First there was St. Mary Falls parking area, then the Gunsight Pass trailhead, and now, Siyeh Bend. As Dad got higher up, it became windy. He worked hard as he fought the elevation gain and the gusty winds. *Just stay in rhythm, don't push too hard*, he reminded himself. Dad lifted one of his arms to wipe the sweat that trickled down his forehead and into his eyes.

As Dad pushed past the Siyeh parking area, he gazed ahead. The morning sunlight was lighting up the park's high peaks. Dad recognized Clements Mountain, its snowfield that was once a glacier illuminated by the bright light. "I'm getting there!" he encouraged himself out loud. Then Dad glanced in the tiny mirror attached to his helmet. He noticed even more smoke billowing into the sky.

• • •

"It's 8 AM," James announced. "Dad should be reaching the top soon."

Morgan, James, and Mom scrambled out of the tent.

"Well, let's start getting everything ready, then," Mom said.

Morgan began preparing pancakes, eggs, and bacon. She set up a cake with candles. James unrolled the banner they had stashed away under their suitcases and camping supplies.

Soon their campsite was all ready for Dad's birthday.

After they were all set, Morgan turned the stove down and covered the food with foil. Mom came over and put her arm around Morgan. James joined them. The three of them surveyed their decorations. "You know, forty is a big milestone!" Mom said. "Dad will be thrilled."

• • •

Dad climbed on. The road was cut into a rocky cliff; on his right the cliff towered above him, on his left it plunged below. Dad crossed a steel bridge and rode next to a pounding waterfall. He pedaled quickly through a dark tunnel. Logan Pass Visitor Center was just up the road.

Dad gained momentum and pedaled with renewed energy. *Am I getting stronger,* he wondered, *or is the road just leveling out?*

Dad noticed a bighorn sheep walking on a cement barrier next to the road. He slowly rode by, trying to avoid eye contact with the noble but ominous-looking animal. *You don't see that on too many bike rides,* he thought to himself.

Then Dad rounded a bend. Two more bighorns stood in the middle of the road. He looked at them, gauging if he could ride past quickly while pedaling uphill.

Dad decided he wasn't fast enough to get by safely. He stopped and waited. A car on the other side of the sheep was also waiting. They noticed Dad. He shrugged his shoulders as if to say, *What else am I supposed to do?*

The bighorns looked at the car, then at Dad. They took a few panicked, erratic steps in random directions. Dad prepared himself to turn the bike around and flee. All of a sudden, without warning, the bighorns ran off the road and scampered up a hill.

Dad took a deep breath and rode on, watching the bighorns above him as he pedaled past.

Finally, he made it to the final pitch, sprinting up the last stretch to the visitor center parking lot. Dad pulled in just as a ranger was putting up a barricade on the road.

Logan Pass Visitor Center's parking lot was mostly empty. Near the bottom end were several ranger cars and fire trucks. Some of the firefighters were talking with each other. One was looking through binoculars to the east. Another spoke into a hand radio.

Dad looked at the newly set up roadblock. A car pulled up to it from the west. The ranger stepped over to the driver as she rolled down her window. "The road is closed," the ranger announced. "The fire has flared up and is running close to the highway. For now, everything east of here is shut down."

The driver backed up and turned around. Meanwhile Dad walked over to the ranger. "My family's down there," he informed him. "At Rising Sun."

"Not for long," the man replied.

• • •

A ranger drove around the campground. She stopped at the Parkers' site and quickly jogged over to Morgan, James, and Mom.

"Hi, folks," she greeted the family while looking at the decorations. "I'm sorry to break up the party, but we're closing the whole area east of Logan Pass. The fires are raging out of control and moving this way."

Mom looked at the ranger in shock. "Now?"

"Now!"

"But my husband's riding his bike on Going-to-the-Sun Road!"

"I'm sorry, ma'am. If he's up at the pass, he'll have to go west. If he's somewhere in between, the rangers sweeping the road will pick him up.

"I'll radio the situation in," she reassured Mom. The ranger hurried back to her car. Then she drove to the next campsite.

Dad rolled over to the fire crew. He waited nearby and watched them discuss the situation. Meanwhile, several other cyclists arrived at the parking lot from the west.

Dad felt a chill from the morning wind and the sweat he had worked up on his climb. He pulled his windbreaker out of his jersey pouch and slipped it on. Then Dad watched the smoke from the fire expanding high into the sky.

The firefighter who had been talking on the radio turned and spoke to his crew. "The wind has shifted and it's become a raging inferno down there. And the fire's getting close to the highway above St. Mary Lake."

Several firefighters hurriedly ran to their vehicles. Two trucks took off to the east; the ranger with the barricade moved it so they could get by.

Dad wondered what Mom and the kids were going through. He wheeled himself a little closer. "Excuse me." A ranger paused. "I just rode my bike up here this morning, and my family's at Rising Sun Campground," Dad informed them. The ranger glanced at Dad, not anticipating this kind of predicament. He held up his hand. "Hang on a moment."

After conferring with the others for a moment, the ranger returned quickly to Dad. "You can't go back down," he said. "It's too dangerous, and the road is already closed."

"What about my family?"

Again the ranger held up his hand so he could discuss the situation further with his crew. Meanwhile, the other bike riders pedaled over to find out what was going on.

• • •

Mom, Morgan, and James hastily broke down camp. Morgan put as much food as she could into containers. Mom and James tore down the tent and stuffed the sleeping bags into their sacks. The three of them threw everything haphazardly into the car and piled in. Mom started up the car, and they headed for the campground exit.

Morgan gazed out the window at the totally obscured sky.

Ashes drifted onto the car like snow. James saw raging flames flickering up the side of a nearby hill. "The fire's really close," he reported nervously.

As they approached the main road, they were met by a patrol car. The ranger there directed all traffic east.

Mom turned the required direction. "We'll find out about Dad as soon as we can," she said.

• • •

From their vantage point at Logan Pass, the group of cyclists stared at the massive bomblike cloud of smoke ballooning up from the horizon.

"The fire's been going on all week," Dad mentioned to the others, "but it's gotten a lot worse since yesterday."

The ranger strode briskly over to the cyclists. "We're sending up a shuttle bus to haul you and your bikes down to the western side of the park. With all the fire crews coming up, there's too much traffic on the road for a safe bike ride. The bus can drop you at Avalanche Creek Campground or anywhere farther west."

Then the ranger looked at Dad. "I suggest you go to Apgar. If your family checks in at St. Mary, we'll inform them through the emergency dispatch that you are there."

The cyclists wheeled over to the bus stop. They all sat down and waited for the shuttle. Dad told the small group about how he got separated from his family. Others told of similar situations. "I'm supposed to meet my family at Rising Sun," one said. "I don't know how we're going to meet up now."

"I wonder where we'll all end up tonight," another added.

• • •

Mom drove east along with a line of evacuating cars. To the south, flames roared up on the other side of St. Mary Lake.

The Parkers approached the visitor center. A ranger stationed there directed all traffic to keep on going.

Once out of the park, Mom pulled over at the intersection. A ranger and fire truck were parked next to a Road Closed sign. Mom, Morgan, and James hurried over to the emergency personnel.

"My husband is on that road with his bike somewhere," she told the ranger anxiously.

"Ah, the bicyclists. We were told about that."

"And?"

"Apparently several cyclists are stuck at the summit."

"So everyone's okay?"

"From what I've heard, yes. They're going to be shuttled down to the west side and have been told to reunite with their families and friends at Apgar."

Mom remembered where Apgar was. "With this road closed, how do we get there?"

"The only way would be to head south to the junction at East Glacier. From there you can pick up Highway 2 along the southern end of the park. But it won't be easy or quick. There's a second fire there, near the highway. It's extremely smoky, and pilot cars are escorting groups through."

"Thanks," Mom said. She put her arms around James and Morgan. "Come on, we've got a long journey ahead."

• • •

The bus came a while later and picked up Dad and the others. As they wound their way down the west side of Going-to-the-Sun Road, a line of fire trucks climbed in the other direction.

One of the cyclists looked at Dad and kindly asked, "Do you need any food?"

"Thanks," Dad replied. "I still have a couple of energy bars. And I also have some money. There's a store at Lake McDonald and at Apgar. I'll be fine."

The bus continued to descend to lower elevations. Eventually the road leveled out. The skies on the west side of the park were surprisingly blue.

The other cyclists exited the bus at Avalanche Creek Campground. "Good luck!" one called out to Dad as he hauled his bike off.

Dad exited the shuttle at Lake McDonald. As he lifted his bike down,

Dad said to the driver, "The rest of the road is mostly flat, so I might as well ride. Thanks for the lift."

Dad watched the bus drive away. Then he hopped on his bike and began pedaling toward Apgar.

In the northern part of the park, a male moose bellowed. It pranced out of the forest and noticed a female and her calf. But there was another male nearby.

The two competitors sized each other up. They stepped forward, then trotted closer. The males collided, grunting while shoving together forcefully. They locked antlers and attempted to push each other back. Both moose breathed heavily and continued to push for further leverage. At different times, each gained and lost steps while adjusting the position of his antlers.

Finally, one of the moose shook his head back and forth, then thrust his antlers forward and knocked the other out of balance. The defeated moose scampered backward and trotted into a nearby marsh.

The dominant moose lifted his head upright and pranced into the vicinity of the female. It pawed and scuffed at the ground, eventually digging out a depression.

The moose stepped out of the hole and walked up to a tree. The bull rubbed his antlers against the trunk, scouring off the new fuzzy growth. He shook his antlers several times, letting bits of fuzz drop off.

The female moose watched the proceedings. Finally, she stepped toward the newly formed den created by the bull.

At the town of East Glacier, Mom turned the car southwest on Highway 2. A few miles later, the Parkers approached a line of cars. Mom pulled up and waited.

Morgan stared out the window. "It's so smoky," she said anxiously, thinking about Dad breathing in the polluted air as he rode his bike. Ashes continued to waft onto the car and pile up while they sat there.

After a thirty-minute delay, a pilot car heading northeast passed with a long line of cars following it. After the last car went by, the pilot car turned around to pull in front of the Parkers' group.

Slowly, the waiting travelers began moving. Soon they were inching along at twenty-five miles per hour on the road paralleling the southern end of the park.

Outside was an eerie fire scene. Fire trucks next to the road blocked one of the lanes. Some were pumping water into the smoldering brush nearby.

Dark, dense smoke choked the whole region. Mom turned on her headlights. Flames flickered on hillsides, and several hot spots flared up right next to the road.

"It looks like a war zone out there," Mom observed worriedly. "But I know the rangers were watching this develop. I'm sure Dad is in a safe place by now."

Suddenly, two dark forms escaped from the smoke and flames and ran onto the highway. "Look," James exclaimed, "wolves!"

The stunned animals froze in the headlights of the cars. One wolf quickly galloped south toward a nonburning forested area. The other limped after his companion.

"That one looks like the one we saw the other day!" Morgan said. "But it's hard to tell with all the smoke."

Soon the wolves had run out of sight.

• • •

Dad pedaled along Going-to-the-Sun Road. Eventually he made it to Apgar and rode up to the visitor center. A bulletin board was posted in front of the building with an update on the fire conditions. Dad read the information and looked at a map. *Kristen and the kids must be here on this highway*, he thought.

Dad put his bike against a wall and walked inside to find out more.

After talking with the rangers, Dad stocked up on snacks at the store across the street to energize himself for the several-mile-long ride up to Fish Creek Campground and whatever easy meal he might need later. He paid for a site near where they had stayed a week ago. Dad pedaled up to it, walked his bike onto the dirt, and sat at the picnic table. Dad stayed there, staring through the trees, thinking about his family and where they might be now and how they would find each other. He looked at the lake and wondered what to do next.

Dad rode back to the campground check-in station, borrowed some paper and a pen, and wrote a quick note:

Hi Kristen, Morgan, and James! I reserved us a campsite—D–18. It's five o'clock right now. I am going to ride back to Apgar and hope to see you there. I'm okay and I hope you are too.
Love,
Dad

Dad anchored the message to the picnic table with a rock and rode back into Apgar Village. He also posted a message on the bulletin board in Apgar. All he could do now was wait.

Dad stayed around the Apgar area watching people come and go. After a while, he walked back to the ranger station and checked for updated information about travel on Highway 2. *It's going to take them some time to get here,* he realized.

Dad wheeled his bike down to the water at Lake McDonald. He sat near the shore and gazed at the surprisingly clear view.

• • •

Mom, Morgan, and James approached a bend in the road at Bear Creek. The pilot car pulled aside and let the caravan of cars pass. Mom followed the car ahead of her into two-way traffic.

"It's less smoky now," James reported.

"Yeah, I feel like I can breathe again," Morgan added with relief in her voice.

"We're going to be fine, kids," Mom assured them. "Look, the cars around us are speeding up. At this rate, hopefully we'll get to Apgar in an hour or so."

• • •

The late afternoon breeze chilled Dad. He zipped up his jacket just as he heard footsteps approaching.

Dad turned and, to his surprise, saw two familiar faces. "Hey! It's my old buddies from Sperry Chalet!"

"Hi!" Greg smiled. "Long time no see."

The couple saw Dad's bike. "Are you out for a spin?" Corinne asked.

"Sort of. But it's not quite the ride I intended it to be."

Dad told Greg and Corinne about his climb up Going-to-the-Sun Road and the closure at the summit.

"So," Corinne said, "you're here without food, your camping supplies, and your family?"

"That's pretty much it."

"Throw your bike in our truck," Greg spontaneously suggested, "and we'll drive you back to Fish Creek Campground."

"Thanks," Dad said. "I've already ridden that stretch of road a couple of times today, and I was getting pretty tired from it."

Greg and Corinne got into the truck, and Dad hoisted his bike into the back. Then he hopped into the backseat to join them.

"We need to stop at the store really quick on the way," Corinne mentioned. "Is that okay?"

"Of course," Dad replied.

• • •

Mom, Morgan, and James drove up to the ranger station. Morgan hopped out of the car and ran up to the building. She first checked the fire information board. Then Morgan jogged to where notes were posted. Morgan found Dad's note. She read it, then ran back to the car.

"Dad made it!" Morgan reported excitedly. "He says he's in site D-18 at Fish Creek. And if he's not there, he's around here somewhere, looking for us."

Mom drove around the block several times. They also checked by the lake. "I think Dad's probably in camp now," Mom concluded after not seeing any bicyclists.

The three Parkers headed toward Fish Creek.

• • •

At the store across the street, Dad grabbed some additional food to supplement his stash.

Greg and Corinne saw Dad's basket as he joined them in line. "You're hungry!" Greg exclaimed.

"A little," Dad admitted. "But now that I don't have to carry all this in my bike jersey, I thought I'd bring it to camp."

"You're going to eat all that tonight?" Corinne inquired.

"Maybe," Dad replied. "I can always save some for morning."

"Where?" Greg asked. "As of now, you have no car to store it in."

"You're right. I hadn't thought about that."

Greg and Corinne looked at each other and nodded. "We've got an idea," Greg said. "We're staying at a hotel just outside the park. We'll hang out with you until dark. If your family isn't there by then, you are welcome to stay with us."

"You don't have to do that," Dad replied sheepishly.

"You can't stay in camp without a tent and sleeping bag!" Greg exclaimed.

"That's really kind of you," Dad said. "Boy, I sure hope Kristen and the twins make it here before nightfall, though!"

Dad paid for his food. They left the store and walked back to the truck. The three got in and began driving to Fish Creek.

• • •

Mom slowed down at the campground entrance station and rolled down her window. "We're the rest of the Parkers in site D-18," she reported.

The woman in the booth looked at a list. "Okay," she replied. "I've got your name here."

The ranger wrote their campsite number on a slip of paper. "Here," she said, handing it to Mom. "Put this in your driver's-side window."

Mom posted the paper, then leaned out. "Have you seen a man on a bike wearing a blue jersey?"

"Yes," the woman replied. "I saw him earlier today."

"Thanks," Mom said with a sigh of relief. She drove through, and they found site D-18, but it was empty. Morgan hopped out of the car and found another note from Dad on the picnic table. She picked it up and dashed back. "I've got another clue!" Morgan called out.

Morgan read the note to Mom and James. "We must have missed him somewhere in Apgar," James concluded.

"Or he's on his way here," Morgan added.

"But then we would have seen him on the road," Mom realized.

"Should we go back?" James asked.

"I've got an idea," Mom said. "In case he's around here somewhere, let's set up for his birthday and wait. Then if we have to, we'll go back."

"Okay," Morgan and James agreed.

The three of them hurriedly got out all their decorations. They taped up the Happy 40th, Dad! banner, put out the tablecloth, Dad's card, and his birthday cake.

Mom grabbed the candles and pushed them into the cake. "Let's get a few pictures now too, before Dad gets here," she suggested.

Morgan found her camera and snapped several photos.

• • •

When Greg, Corinne, and Dad drove up to the campground entrance station, Dad leaned out the window behind Greg and asked the attendant, "Has anyone checked into D-18?"

The woman in the booth smiled. "Yes. They just got here a few minutes ago!"

Dad raised his arms. "Yeah!" he called out.

• • •

Mom gazed at their site with James and Morgan. "It looks festive, doesn't it? But we're still missing one thing."

"Dad!" they all said at once.

A truck drove up. Morgan, James, and Mom stared at it. They saw a couple in the front, but didn't recognize them.

Morgan noticed there was a bike in the bed of the truck. First Greg got out, then Corinne. Finally, a man climbed out of the backseat.

"Dad!" James and Morgan called out, running up to their father.

"Honey!" Mom exclaimed and joined in the reunion.

Dad hugged and kissed his family. Then he stepped back and inspected their campsite. "You've been busy!"

"Wait!" Mom said. She lit the candles and called everyone over, including Greg and Corinne. "Okay, ready everyone?"

And they all started singing.

"Happy Birthday to you…"

Dad blew out his candles, looked up, and smiled. "My wish already came true."

"What did you wish?" Morgan asked.

"I don't want to say. That would jinx it. But I bet you can guess."

Mom looked at Greg and Corinne. "You're going to stay for cake, right?"

"Of course," Corinne replied. She looked at Dad. "Why didn't you tell us it was your birthday?"

"I had other things on my mind."

After eating, the Parkers exchanged addresses with Greg and Corinne.

As the couple walked back to their truck, Greg called out, "We'll e-mail you our pictures from Sperry Glacier!"

"I'll send you ours!" Morgan called back.

Once Greg and Corinne were gone, Dad smiled at his family. "Come here, all of you."

Dad put his arms around Morgan, James, and Mom. "Thank you for a great birthday! It really was a surprise."

"We had it set up for you at Rising Sun," Morgan informed him.

"Really?" Dad replied.

"Yes," James said. "After you took off this morning, we set it all up."

"Then we had to take it down once we were evacuated," Morgan added.

The Parkers cleaned up. Afterward, Dad noticed it was still light out. "How about a little walk to the lake?" he suggested.

The family strolled down to the same beach they had visited over a week ago. Morgan and James brought along their journals.

They all sat down in the sand. The skies were clouding up, but to the east a gigantic plume of smoke towered over the park's high mountains.

"Hey," James realized, "we never made it to the Two Medicine area."

"That leaves us something to come back for," Dad said.

While the family sat in silence, Morgan pulled out her journal.

Dear Diary:

It's our last night in Glacier. We're camped again at Fish Creek, which feels kind of like our old home.

We've had a crazy day! Dad rode his bike up Going-to-the-Sun Road, but they wouldn't let him come back down. They shut the road because of a huge fire. So we couldn't get to Dad, and he couldn't get back to us!

Mom, James, and I then had to drive all the way around the park to get to Apgar. Dad was shuttled down here. And this is where we had our reunion. I was really worried for a while, but everything turned out fine.

But what a drive through the fire area we had on Highway 2! The smoke and flames were so close to us, at times we could feel the heat radiating through the car. I don't think I'll ever forget that experience.

And I'll never forget Glacier! Here are my top ten sights in the park:

1. Sexton Glacier—Siyeh Pass Trail
2. The mountain goats on Hidden Lake Trail
3. Grinnell Glacier and Lake
4. Going-to-the-Sun Road
5. The moose at Kootenai Lake
6. Sperry Chalet
7. Sperry Glacier
8. Avalanche Lake and its waterfalls
9. Bowman Lake
10. The wolf at Two Dog Flats

Mom says, "Glacier might be the best place in the world."

I know I'm coming back.

Until next time,

Morgan

James stared at the lake a little longer, then pulled out his journal.

This is James Parker reporting from Glacier National Park in northern Montana. What I'm going to remember most about this fantastic place is that the glaciers are disappearing. They say that in about ten years—when Morgan and I are in college—there won't be any left! Can't we do something to slow down global warming!? The ranger at Logan Pass said driving less, eating locally grown foods, and using energy-efficient appliances at home can help.

My top ten sights are mostly in honor of Glacier's glaciers, although I saw many other great things in the park.

1. Grinnell Glacier and the iceberg that broke off
2. Gem and Salamander glaciers
3. Piegan and Sexton glaciers
4. Sperry Glacier and the chalet
5. Blackfoot and Jackson glaciers
6. The boat tour on Waterton Lake
7. The views at Gunsight Pass
8. The marmot in the storm cabin
9. Seeing the bear dogs at the Swiftcurrent Motor Inn parking lot
10. Polebridge townsite and Bowman Lake

Reporting from Glacier National Park,

James Parker

James put down his journal and sighed.

Mom noticed James's somber mood. "What's wrong?" she asked.

"I'm sad that we're leaving."

"Me too," Morgan added.

"Me too!" Dad said.

The Parkers huddled close in the slowly fading evening light. A few drops of water began plunking down. James looked up. "Hey, it's raining!"

The scattered clouds spit out a few more drops.

"Maybe this will help the fires," Morgan said.

"Maybe," Mom replied. "But they'll need a heck of a lot more than this."

Dad looked up at the nearly dark sky. "Come on, rain!" he shouted.

The family stood up and slowly trudged back to camp. "Better get some rest," Mom said while yawning. "We've got a long drive home to California tomorrow."

It was a rainy late autumn day in the central

California coastal town of San Luis Obispo. Morgan and James were off from school for Thanksgiving break.

As James surfed the Internet, his thoughts drifted back to Glacier.

He left his computer and wandered over to Morgan's room. Her door was open. "Can I borrow your CD of Glacier pictures?"

Morgan stood up. "Sure. Can I look at them with you?"

Morgan put their CD photo album into her computer. Together, she and James sifted through pictures of their summer vacation. "It makes me a little homesick for the park," Morgan said.

After looking at a few more pictures, James walked back to his room. He sat at his desk and stared out the window at the rain dripping down. *Weather*, James thought.

James's class had recently studied weather, and he knew some websites to check. James pulled one up on the Internet and clicked on the Glacier region. He scrolled down for a local forecast of the area.

One of the radar maps had a blue coloring over Glacier Park. "Yeah!" James called out.

A moment later, Morgan walked into James's room. "What's going on? I heard you yell."

"It's snowing in Glacier."

James showed Morgan the precipitation map of Montana. "I wonder if the fires are all out now," he said.

"Or if the snow is replenishing the glaciers?" Morgan said.

"I wonder what the bears and wolves are doing," James said. "Are they hibernating?"

"Or if that moose will have another calf," Morgan added.

Meanwhile, back in Glacier, a husky, brown furry animal scampered through a fresh layer of snow, leaving behind a winding trail of prints.

The animal rushed along, her keen sense of smell alerting her she was near a source of food. The carnivore lowered her nose and sniffed.

The pregnant wolverine voraciously started pawing away at the snow and shoveling it backwards in a spray of powdery ice. The fierce animal dug further until she had reached bare ground and the remnant bones of a moose calf.

The wolverine bit into a bone, easily snapping it with her powerful jaws and sharp teeth. She held the bone in place with a paw and devoured the whole leg, including the nutritious marrow...